D1591240

THE HACKER

RENEE ROSE

BURNING DESIRES

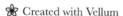 Created with Vellum

WANT FREE RENEE ROSE BOOKS?

Go to http://subscribepage.com/alphastemp to sign up for Renee Rose's newsletter and receive a free copy of *Alpha's Temptation, Theirs to Protect, Owned by the Marine, Theirs to Punish, The Alpha's Punishment, Disobedience at the*

Dressmaker's and *Her Billionaire Boss*. In addition to the free stories, you will also get bonus epilogues, special pricing, exclusive previews and news of new releases.

PROLOGUE

ST. PETERSBURG 2011

Dima

I slam the brakes on the Lada too hard, sending the car I share with my twin brother into a full spin on the icy highway. For one glorious moment, I think I've done it.

I've ended things. I won't have to sell my soul to the bratva to repay the loan I took for her treatment.

I'm going to join her. I promised there'd be no one else for me. I swore it there in the hospital, the night before she took her last breath. When she took off the ring I gave her and put it on my pinkie finger.

You are always mine, and I am always yours. Even in death.

Wait for me. I'll be there soon.

Right before I went home and beat my bedroom wall until it crumbled.

Nikolai's frantic yells fill my ears as our car smashes into a guardrail, crushing my side of the car in. Metal screams, glass shatters. We teeter on the side of a bridge over a frozen river. This is it. Time to die. The pain will end now.

1

I don't know if I believe in an afterlife, but I do know I don't want to live without her.

Nikolai unbuckles his seat belt and throws his door open, yanking me by the shirt to haul me out on his side.

"*Nyet.*" I don't move. The moment he gets out, the car will fall to the river below. I don't know if the ice will break beneath the weight. Maybe the impact alone will kill me. I can only hope.

Nikolai keeps hold of my shirt with one hand. With the other, he punches me in the face.

Pain explodes in my nose and behind my eyes. My vision goes black, blood pours into my mouth.

Nikolai uses my disorientation to yank me from behind the wheel. "Get the hell out," he growls in Russian.

My vision still hasn't returned. My legs scramble—fuck. I think they're helping me climb out.

I throw out a hand to grab for the door handle. The steering wheel. Something to keep me in the car when it slides off the bridge, but my twin is too fast. He throws his weight backward and falls down to the ground outside his door, pulling me on top of him.

Metal groans. The car teeters and then slides away from us. For a moment, it feels as if the bridge itself is falling, as world swoops around me. And then it crashes to the river below.

Nikolai punches me in the face again. And again. "You don't get to die today, asshole." Another punch. "And you don't get to fucking bring me with you."

I groan, choking on blood.

I didn't mean to kill Nikolai. I am a bastard for not even separating myself from him.

I hadn't planned on dying tonight—not consciously, anyway. But I should have given his presence in the car more thought before I executed that non-plan.

That's the thing with twins. Nikolai feels like an extension of myself. The silent presence who shared my pain through the months of Alyona's chemo and radiation. Who did my homework for me and swapped classes to pretend to be me and take my tests when I stopped caring about school.

He was the guy who found out about the bratva loan when it seemed like a new expensive treatment option might help.

We don't talk about it. We don't need to. He's been with me through the whole fucking thing. From falling in love with the most beautiful girl in the city to putting her in the ground.

I groan and curl up on my side in the snow, turning it crimson with the blood from my nose and the split in my lip.

"Get up."

I don't move.

Over the howling wind, I fail to notice the arrival of another car. A door being thrown open.

"Get in," an authoritative voice commands.

Nikolai tries to haul me up. I don't move.

"Get them in the car."

Two pairs of gleaming black boots stomp around me, and I'm hauled to my feet and shoved in the back of a limo.

That was the night we first met Igor Antonov.

The night the bratva found us and took their due, not in the form of a beat-down or threats, but full ownership of our lives. Because Igor recognized the value of young men with a deathwish. His army was made up of them.

So our mother did lose both her sons that night. She believed we were lost to the icy river, not to the brotherhood that required we disavow all ties to her.

Dima

There you are, beautiful.

Hacking and cyberstalking isn't just a job, it's a way of life. Sitting behind my screen in the penthouse I share with my bratva brothers, I rule the cyberworld. Right now, I'm watching the live security cam feed on our building to glimpse the slender female figure enter the front door and walk to the elevator.

I sprout a semi just seeing her unassuming yet somehow sensual walk and the absent smile that tugs at her lips, like she's thinking of something that makes her happy.

"Who are you spying on?" Nikolai asks from the couch.

Fucker. My twin knows exactly who I'm stalking, and his awareness is becoming more and more of a thorn in my side.

"Ooh, is it a woman?" our roommate, Sasha, calls from the kitchen, then sprints through the living room to look over my shoulder.

Case in point.

I click away before she can see anything, sending both her and Nikolai a glare.

Wrong move. My out-of-character response showed my hand. I should've played it casual.

Sasha gasps theatrically—always the thespian. "It *is* a woman! Who? Let me see." She tries to snatch at my mouse.

"It's your mother," I say then instantly regret it because Sasha's broad smile wobbles and falls. Her greedy mother was involved in a scheme to steal Sasha's inheritance and isn't well-liked around here.

"Wait, really?"

"No. Bad joke. Sorry."

"What the fuck?" Maxim snaps from the kitchen. He doesn't appreciate anyone offending his new bride, which is understandable.

"Sorry." I hold the mouse in the air, out of her reach, but she's still trying to grab it. "Tell your wife not to touch my equipment."

Sasha giggle-snorts.

"That came out wrong. Just move away." I make a shooing motion.

Sasha folds her arms over her chest. "You have to show us now. There's no way I'm backing off until we see."

Knowing there's nothing to see by now—my quarry will be safely in the elevator by now, I set the mouse down. "Fine. This is what I was watching." I click back on the feed, which shows the screen of the front lobby of our building, Maykl sitting behind the desk, less doorman than our heavily armed sentry.

Cyberstalking is my entertainment, my window to the world, my identity. With a keyboard and screen, I'm god. I consider my view of all data a right I earned by knowing how to access it.

Everyone's business is my business because it's all there for me to see. I can find every scrap of data about them. I can reshuffle it, rearrange it to change their lives with a few strokes of my keys. I can get them in trouble with the IRS, I can wipe their police records clean. I can change their credit score, steal their identity.

"Kuznets wants your help with a hacking project," my boss, Ravil, mentions as he passes through the living room. "I gave him your number. He's going to have Sergei Litvin call you from Moscow."

"Okay."

I hoped Ravil's interruption would distract Sasha, but she's still after me. "So it's someone in the building?" she demands. "Who?"

"Who indeed?" Nikolai murmurs, a sardonic edge to his voice.

This time, I'm smart and ignore him.

Sasha whirls to pin Nikolai with her gaze. "Is it a woman?" She gives an Oscar-worthy gasp. "Is it Natasha?"

"Is it?" Nikolai asks blandly, shifting his gaze to me.

"Why would I stalk Natasha?" I scoff but even saying her name out loud does something to me.

Because I'm always stalking the very lovely Natasha Zolotova, the sexy-as-hell, jail-bait daughter of one of the residents in our building who gives me a hard-on simply by existing. She's not actually jail-bait. She's twenty-three— about the same age as Sasha. But she has this fresh-faced sweetness that makes her seem like she could be eighteen. She's the proverbial girl next door. She brings cheer to the entire building.

Of course, I already know everything there is to know about her. I keep tabs on everyone in the building as part of my job for Ravil, the bratva boss who provides my twin brother and I a very comfortable life within the confines of the brotherhood.

But stalking Natasha is a daily activity for me, along with washing my face and brushing my teeth. Out of respect, I don't read her emails or listen to her calls. I just like to check her Instagram photos. Watch the video feed from our building's security cameras showing her coming in and out. I like to know what she's wearing. Her mood. That she's safe. I like to know how often she works—not enough to move out of her mother's apartment or be able to support herself, as far as I can tell.

Today she's in a melon-colored halter top over yoga pants, a fact I will verify in person in a few moments. I watch as she enters the apartment she shares with her mom, then comes back out, rolling her massage table to the elevator.

I close my laptop and stand.

"You have somewhere to be?" Nikolai asks.

I am seriously going to kill the guy. I flip him the bird as I walk out of the penthouse suite, around the elevator to where I have a single bedroom that opens to the hallway, hotel room style.

My dick gets hard knowing Natasha will be getting off that elevator and knocking at my door in just a minute, her beautiful face doing crazy things to my resolve. I step inside my room and lean my forehead against the door.

The elevator dings. I try to get my thoughts out of the gutter.

I hate that she's a mobile massage therapist—she brings her table to other people's houses. It's dangerous as hell. She told me she doesn't see anyone she doesn't know personally or who hasn't been personally recommended, and she also told me she doesn't see men, but I know that's bullshit, since she's given me two massages and will be up here shortly to give me another.

I made her promise if anyone ever messed with her she'd tell me. I may not be huge and able to snap necks with one hand like Oleg, our enforcer, but I'd damn well be lethal if anyone hurt that girl.

Not that she's mine to protect. As much as I enjoy stalking Natasha, that's all I will do.

Booking the massages—that was a mistake. A huge one.

It was Nikolai's fault. My asshole twin must've noted my, er, *dedication* to keeping tabs on her, so he threatened to book a massage, himself, if I wouldn't. And there was no way I'd let Nikolai be naked in the same room as Natasha.

No *fucking* way.

So now I have to suffer through *me* being naked in the same room as Natasha and having those sweet hands touch me everywhere—well, almost everywhere—and not have my dick in my fist. *Gospodi*, I'm harder than marble the entire hour, and it's the worst kind of torture. Especially when she flirts with me.

I'm not usually the guy women are attracted to. Nikolai gets them with his charm and general air of danger. Pavel, Ravil, Oleg, and Maxim—the other guys in our bratva cell —they all have women throwing panties their way—or at least they did before they claimed their current partners.

Me, though?

I'm the computer geek. The hacker.

I'm not charming because I don't even try. I'm the guy behind the curtain, manipulating the scenes from a computer screen.

But for some reason, Natasha seems to like me. Maybe she can sense my attraction to her—women are intuitive that way. She looks up at me with big sea green eyes like

I'm someone worth having, and it shreds me from the inside.

Because I'm not.

I'm definitely not worth having.

And more than that, I'm not available.

Natasha

I use a keycard in the gleaming elevator to get to the top floor of the Kremlin, the high rise on Lake Michigan that houses most of the Russians who live in Chicago, including myself. Like every time I come to the top floor, my pulse quickens. Before the doors open, I put on fresh lip gloss and fluff my hair. Today I'm on a mission.

I shouldn't have access to the penthouse floor, but Dima gave me this card when he booked his first massage with me. I thought it meant something at the time. The tattooed bratva member had been so attentive every time I'd been in his suite, working for his boss.

But then he rescheduled. And rescheduled again.

Four times.

And then the two times I gave him a massage, he acted stiff and stand-offish. So yeah, my hopes for something happening between me and the hot bad boy on the top floor have gradually dwindled to nothing.

I roll my massage table out of the elevator and stand in front of his door now, lifting my hand to knock. He opens it before my knuckles hit the wood. *"Amerikanka."*

He calls me *American.* It seems like a friendly-enough moniker, but I'm not sure. It could be a dig. I think it's a joke because I've fully integrated into American society. I worked hard to expunge the Russian accent from my speech. No one who met me would know I didn't move here until I was nine.

"Hi." Butterflies flap their wings in my tummy at the sight of him. He's tall, lanky and blond. His black-framed glasses and friendly face make him look more GQ than street thug.

But he *is* a street thug, as my mother just reminded me by phone before I came up here. None of these men are safe, and they are definitely not for me, according to her rules.

Dima wears a worn *Matrix* t-shirt and a faded pair of jeans. His hair is rumpled, like he's been shoving his fingers through it. He's not beefy, but he has lowkey muscles, despite being a computer geek. *IT Specialist* is the official title, but I'd bet my last penny on him being a hacker. One of Russia's finest, no doubt. The guy is always at a computer, and he seems hella smart.

"Hey." He scowls at the massage table like it's an unruly dog. Snatching it out of my grasp, he carries it in.

"It has wheels, you know." I follow him in. I try to banter, to put him at ease the way he used to do for me when I came up to massage his boss's wife during her pregnancy, but when I'm in his room, when we're alone, I never see that easy-going smile or joking banter of his. Instead, he almost seems defensive. Like he's mad at me over something.

He doesn't respond.

"Or did you just want to show off your superior strength?" When he doesn't answer, just starts unzipping the bag like he's the therapist and I'm the client, I add, "I'm already well-acquainted with your muscles, you know."

Yes, I'm shameless with my flirting. It's because he never does anything about it! I could have sworn this guy liked me. I thought he was asking me to massage him as an opening to… more.

And no, I'm not *that kind* of massage therapist. I don't do happy endings. But I could have sworn Dima was interested. Anytime I was in the main penthouse suite, his gaze would follow me. Sometimes there was a light touch—his hand at my lower back, like we were on a date.

And then the most glaring evidence: his hard-ons during the two massages I've given him. The tension he never releases. It's like the guy suffers through my sessions instead of relaxing and enjoying them.

But he never asks me out or flirts back. I even tried asking *him* out, very casually. I asked if he was going to see his roommate's band play at Rue's Lounge. He said no, then showed up, didn't speak to me, and glared at everyone who talked to me. And when I say everyone, I don't even mean guys hitting on me. I was sitting with his suitemates —the members of his bratva cell and one of their wives.

After that, I stopped waiting. Stopped expecting him to do anything about it. And I should stop flirting because I started seeing a guy a few weeks ago. A hot half-Russian guy who just started as a personal trainer at my gym.

I pull out the sheets and cover the table, turn on my massage music, and get out the oil. "I'll just wait behind the door while you get undressed and lie facedown on the table," I say in my best quiet spa voice. I swear I feel Dima's gaze on my ass as I walk into the bathroom—the only place to go to give him privacy in his hotel-room-like bedroom setup. I wait until the rustling sounds go quiet and then knock before I come out.

I pull the sheet down to expose his back. All of the bratva members have tattoos. Some are the same, some are different. I've memorized every one of Dima's, which I find the most fascinating. Most of the bratva guys' tattoos are crude, probably made in prison with a penknife and ink from a broken pen. Dima sports colorful art down both his arms. Across his right shoulder blade and down his right biceps are a series of ones and zeros. Computer code. That's why I'm banking on him being a hacker. The bratva's tattoos depict their crimes. Their stints in prison. Their initiations to the brotherhood. Who they served. How long they've served. At least that's what I've surmised. I know better than to ask.

I focus on his right shoulder to start with—it's always the tightest, not that he ever complains. This probably sounds weird, but I relish touching Dima. He may not enjoy my massages, but I sure as hell enjoy giving them. I like the feel of his muscles under my palms. The scent of his aftershave, his stoic silence.

Today, like the other times I've massaged him, his hips go cockeyed the moment I touch him, a boner tilting his pelvis. It can't be comfortable. If I were the bolder, fearless version of myself, I would lean down and with a purr in his ear, ask if he wanted me to work out that particular part of his anatomy.

But that's not me. I'm not a sex-kitten. I'm just friendly, helpful Natasha, here to serve with a smile.

I work out the muscles of his deltoid and biceps then down his forearm to his fingers. Holding his hand makes the flutters start in my tummy again. Like the hands are a more intimate body part than all the other places I'm touching. Dima wears a slender gold band with a diamond chip on his pinkie finger. I'm guessing it means something to him because it doesn't go with the rest of him. He's not flashy, not the jewelry wearing type. I work down each finger individually. He has three X's tattooed on his knuckles. All the guys on the top floor have them. I'm guessing they represent kills.

"So, I hear your brother runs a Friday night poker game." I don't know why my heart starts pounding so hard. It's a little awkward, but all I have to do is get an invite to the game. This is my mission.

Alex, my new guy, really wants to go. He got super interested when he heard I lived in the Kremlin. I guess he'd heard about the game.

Dima stiffens even more than he was. When he doesn't answer, I plow forward.

"May I come?"

"No," he says immediately. His voice is thick and gruff.

"No?" I laugh to cover my embarrassment. I'd pretty much promised Alex I could get us in. "Why not?"

"Natasha, those games are for serious betters. Not you."

"Maybe I want to seriously bet." Now I'm just annoyed. What is with this guy anyway? My mission morphs from being for Alex to proving I'm not a total loser.

"No." His voice sounds even harder.

"Well, can I come and just watch?" Call me persistent. I adjust the sheet. "Roll over, please."

Dima rolls over.

"Please?" I say in my sweetest voice. I don't know why I can't take no for an answer. I personally have no interest in the game, and it's not like I'm trying to impress Alex. I actually don't think we have a future. He feels more brotherly than boyfriend. I think I'm just hurt that Dima told me no, and that, combined with his refusal to act on his obvious interest in me, makes me rather desperate for a win.

"Natasha…" He scrubs a hand over his face. "I can't believe you're asking me."

I pump some oil into my hands and rub his shoulder

from the top. "Are there, like, strippers there or something?"

Dima snorts. "No strippers."

"Drugs?"

"No drugs."

"Can I just come and check it out? Just once? Please?"

Dima groans and closes his eyes. A moment later, he peeks and catches me watching his face. "Ugn. Fine. Yes, you can come. I'll text you the address."

"Yay! Thank you. I'll be good, I promise." Now I'm flirting again.

Dima cracks one eye, and the sheet tents between his legs.

My heart trips over itself like I'm running down a hill.

Now is when I should tell him I'm bringing Alex. I should definitely tell him now.

Gah. Why don't I want to tell him?

And then I realize the ridiculous truth. The whole reason I agreed to ask Dima if we could go to this game was not to please Alex. It was to show up with Alex and make Dima jealous. Maybe spur him into taking action with me.

I ignore the little prickle at the back of my neck that tells me this is totally going to backfire.

2

Dima

"You did *what?*" Nikolai's head nearly spins off his neck.

I'm set up in my corner of the luxury Chicago hotel suite where tonight's poker game will be held. Nikolai's the bookie. The games are his operation. I'm here to track the bets, vet the players digitally, and run security footage.

Oleg, our bratva cell's enforcer, is here as muscle. He sits in the opposite corner, near the door.

"I gave Natasha the address. She wanted to come," I repeat.

"What. The actual. Fuck?" Nikolai gapes at me. "Seriously. What were you thinking?"

Oleg glances up, but doesn't comment, which isn't unusual. He's mute, and while we've all been learning sign language to understand him, he still doesn't have much to say, except to Story, his girlfriend.

I close my eyes and shove my fingers through my hair. "I know. I tried to refuse her, but she kept begging. I don't know why she wants to come, but she does."

"Her mother will kill us both—and Ravil," he says, mentioning our *pakhan, t*he boss of the Chicago bratva. "You know that woman is not afraid of any of us."

"Svetlana is fierce," I agree. "But she's in Russia at the moment. That's probably why Natasha timed her request now."

"It's not going to work," Nikolai says. "She'll ruin the vibe. I'm not letting her in."

I grit my teeth. Nikolai and I are both generally easygoing, but I've been on edge the last month, and it has everything to do with the little strawberry blonde vixen putting those oiled hands all over my body.

I can't sleep at night. I can't think of anything but stalking her during the days.

"You're letting her in." I give him a hard stare to make sure he sees I mean it.

There's not much I put my foot down about, but anything to do with Natasha makes me cranky. And Nikolai denying her entrance somewhere she wants to be? Not gonna happen.

A muscle twitches in Nikolai's jaw. "You are such a *mudak.* How many months have you been stringing this girl along? You won't even ask her out. *That's* why she asked to come to this game. She's trying to get past your resistance. Are you so fucking blind you can't see it?"

My fingers clench in a fist over my keyboard. The thin band of Alyona's ring bites into my skin on my little finger, the reminder of why I will never ask Natasha out. I want to throw something at my brother.

I refuse to even consider whether he's right.

Natasha and I are not going to happen.

Ever.

I made a promise to Alyona, and I don't break my promises.

"I'm not letting her in," Nikolai repeats stubbornly.

I stand from my workstation. Oleg shifts forward in his chair like he's ready to break up a fight if we throw down over a woman who's not even my girlfriend. "She's already in. I invited her. End of fucking story."

Nikolai frowns at me, nostrils flaring. "Fine," he says after a moment. "But when I give you the signal, you get her the fuck out of here. Understood?"

I hesitate. Of course, I know Nikolai's right. Natasha is the opposite of the kind of player we want. She will turn our serious high-stakes poker game into something low-stakes and frivolous. We won't make any money. Worse, the regulars will be pissed at the interruption of the usual vibe.

I nod. "*Da.*"

Oleg sits back in his chair again.

"You think this is weird, right?" Nikolai asks Oleg. We're doing a better job including him in conversations these days, now that his girlfriend, Story, has forced him to interact more.

Oleg shrugs, but nods, shooting me an apologetic look.

"Yeah, I know," I concede.

Nikolai switches on the background music. A tap sounds at the door, and Oleg opens it, letting Adrian, one of our soldiers in. He's been serving as bartender since Pavel decided to move to L.A. to be with his girl.

Adrian gets to work, unpacking and arranging bottles of liquor on the table provided by the hotel. When Cari, the woman Nikolai hires to deal the cards shows up, I'm reminded of why Natasha shouldn't be welcome here.

Cari is great. Smart, keeps her mouth shut and is a great dealer. But she's in a slinky leopard-print dress with cut-outs on both sides.

Natasha will probably show up in her jeans and a fitted

t-shirt. She has the quintessential American teen look, even though she's not American or a teen.

I settle into my work station—the place I'm most comfortable. If I had it my way—I'd never have to interact with the outside world. I'd just stay in the Kremlin, operating from a keyboard and a screen to manipulate my environment.

Within a half an hour, the knocks start coming on the door.

Zane shows up first. He's a douchy twenty-one-year-old college student. Smart kid, goes to Northwestern. He has a lot of talent. Last year he paid his entire year's tuition with his gambling winnings. But now he's lost his edge. One of our *mudak* players introduced him to the wonders of strip clubs and blow, and now the guy has lost focus.

Nikolai shakes his head at him. "You're not welcome here tonight, Zane, except to make payment on your note. You're down fifty grand." He tips his head toward Oleg, who does the slow rise from his chair. "You're about two days shy of getting a visit from Oleg."

Oleg clenches and unclenches his hand, showing off his meaty fist. The guy is huge, so his size and silence alone are usually deterrent enough for any would-be trouble-makers.

The guy frantically pats the pockets of his black suit jacket. "I brought payment. I did. I have ten grand here." He produces an envelope of cash and thrusts it toward Nikolai who doesn't move. He changes his angle to thrust it toward Oleg, who also doesn't move.

He opens the envelope and starts counting the cash outloud to show Nikolai. When he's done, Nikolai nods and writes it down in his ledger. "You're still not playing tonight."

"Aw, come on, guys." Zane spreads his hands, drops his

head to the side, and turns on the charm. He's privileged and smart and generally good-looking. I'm sure he's used to getting most anything he wants. But it's obvious he's hurtling quickly toward all that potential crashing and burning in a horrible way. "You know I'm good for it. I'll probably make it all back tonight. You know how much I made last year."

"You can't borrow against last year's earnings, my friend. You've lost focus." Nikolai drops a brotherly hand on his shoulder. "Clean your shit up. Keep your nose out of the blow. You're a fucking mess."

Some of the charm frays. Desperation starts to show around the edges as he speaks too fast. "Nikolai, I'm your most loyal client. You know me. You know I can win back what I owe you and more."

"Get out. I need at least another fifteen grand before you sit down at my table again. Now move, or Oleg will throw you off the fucking balcony."

Zane pales and stumbles back toward the door. "All right, all right," he whines. "I'm leaving."

"That one is heading for trouble," I remark when the door closes.

"I predict a spectacular mess," Nikolai agrees.

Over the next twenty-five minutes, the players show up and Nikolai greets them, working the room, making them comfortable, so they'll spend a lot of money.

I can't decide if I'm glad or pissed when it seems like Natasha isn't going to show. I told her to come on time, or she wouldn't get dealt in.

But then the door opens, and I spill my fucking drink down my pantleg. Because Natasha looks gorgeous. Her red hair is in curls across her shoulders, and she's wearing heels and a black halter dress that shows off every fucking curve of her luscious body.

But that's not the part that makes me spill my drink.

It's the asshole she comes in with.

"This is Alex," she's saying to Nikolai. "He's my date."

Her what now?

No. Fucking. Way.

Natasha did not bring a date to our high-stakes poker game.

I get up and walk over, snatching the driver's license Nikolai asked Alex to produce from his fingers. I don't say *hi* or *how-do-you-do* to Natasha.

No fucking way.

I'm beyond pissed.

It's utterly irrational, I know. But so was me telling her she could come to this game.

Everything when it comes to Natasha is irrational.

My need to be near her at the same time I want her to move to Antarctica.

Letting her touch me when every second is torture.

Showing her what I want when I know I won't ever take it.

I stalk to my computer and call up the info on this guy. Everything checks out. Alex is employed by a local gym as a trainer. Graduated from Illinois State. Wrestled in college. He's got a Russian last name—Vasiliev. I don't like that. Not for any particular reason. I mean, it makes sense Natasha might be drawn to another Russian, especially one like her—an Americanized one. But it feels like another red flag.

Not that there was a first one.

Other than him showing up. With *our Natasha*.

Why the fuck did he show up? Was *he* the reason Natasha asked to come to this game?

That thought sends alarm bells ringing, and I start digging into this guy's past even further.

I'm so preoccupied, I miss keeping track of the bets in the first game. I look over and realize Natasha isn't even playing. Just this asshole Alex. She's his arm candy. His fucking lucky rabbit's foot. Nikolai's glares are enough to peel the fancy wallpaper from the walls behind me.

Ya znayu, I mutter aloud to him. *I know.*

I definitely fucked up.

The way that Alex's eyes ping-pong between us makes me think he understood.

"A ty govorish' po russki?" I ask him if he speaks Russian.

"Da, moya mama iz rossii," he answers. *My mother is Russian.*

Why does that make me just hate him all the more? I keep digging, looking for his mother. It takes a while. You know in television shows where the hacker just touches their computer and produces the answer to any and every question? Well, it's not like that. Hacking is time consuming, and you have to know what you're looking for and where to look for it. I've already hacked and given myself permanent access to most databases—the motor vehicle department, police department records, Internal Revenue Service. FBI is harder because I have to re-hack it every thirty days, but I can get in there, too.

I find his mother's name, but no current address or tax filings. Nothing on a father, at all. Alex is a U.S. citizen, born here in Chicago twenty-four years ago.

What an asshole.

I try the FBI. I search for his name in there, and nothing comes up. I search for Ravil's name. I've seen these files before. They don't have much on him. The incident where they tried to turn Lucy, his wife, after he'd kidnapped her and held her hostage at the Kremlin.

And there it is.

An active tag assigned to an agent Alex Volkov. Huh.

That name is suspiciously similar to Alex Vasiliev. I pull up his photo. Yep. Same asshole.

I text Nikolai. I want to text Oleg and Adrian, too, but all three of their phones beeping at once would be a huge tell. Instead, I manage to catch Oleg's eye. I'm about to use my limited sign language to fingerspell F-B-I, but Nikolai says, "hold up," and stops the game.

He stands and walks around to the opposite side of the table as Alex. "What'd you say your last name was?" he asks Alex.

I watch Natasha's face closely.

If I find out she's part of this shit, I will not recover. I don't see fear, just mild confusion.

Dammit.

I need to get her out of this room if things go south. Besides, she owes me a fucking explanation.

I get up, too, and walk over to her side.

Alex is sweating, talking fast, answering Nikolai. I flash a warning glance at Oleg at the same time I hook my hand around Natasha's upper arm and haul her to her feet. "We need to have a word."

The sudden movement beside Alex coupled with being made must cause him to completely lose his head because the asshole fires a shot from below the table, hitting Nikolai in the gut.

Natasha screams. My twin doubles over in a sickening lurch.

"*Nikolai!*" I roar, rage and fear fusing into an adrenaline cocktail that turns me lethal. I kick the table over, thinking to provide protection for Nikolai on the floor if Alex fires again, but Oleg's already there, knocking Alex out with the butt of a gun.

"Oh Jesus, oh fuck," one of the players chants as he

and the rest of the players scramble to their feet and back up.

Adrian points a gun, first at Alex, then looping around the room.

"Put it away," I order. "Get everyone out of here before the cops show. Use the back stairs. *Now.*"

I run to Nikolai's side and crouch down. He's still conscious, but he's bleeding a lot. I throw his arm around my shoulders and struggle to bring us both to our feet.

"Don't kill him," I warn Oleg, who's searching Alex's unconscious form. Not that I have to tell him that. He doesn't kill frivolously or without orders. "Leave him here for the Feds to take care of." Oleg nods and helps Adrian herd the players out of the room.

Natasha's flattened herself against the wall by the door, her green eyes wide, her face drained of color. "Wh-what happened?" she has the nerve to ask me.

"Move it. You're coming with me," I tell her harshly, lifting my chin toward the door.

Her fingers scramble on the handle, and then she throws the door open wide, sending a skittish glance over her shoulder as she scoots out.

"Elevator." I say the word like a curse. Like I could punish her with the tone of my voice alone.

I can't believe what she's done to me.

My brother's been shot.

All because of her. Because I trusted her.

She presses the button over and over again until the elevator arrives, and the three of us step in.

Nikolai's steps are clumsy, and he's heavy on my shoulder, but he's awake, a goofy grin on his face. "I can't believe that fucker shot me," he mutters as the elevator door shuts. "I seriously doubt that was the procedure he learned at Quantico."

"Why… I don't understand," Natasha whimpers.

"Shut up," I snap. "Now listen to me. You are going to get on the other side of Nikolai and wrap your arm around his waist. Put your purse in front of the blood. When those doors open, you're going to walk out with a big fucking smile on your face, like we're all going out to eat together. Got it?"

"Yeah." Her face is pale, and she sounds breathless. "I've got it."

The doors ding and open. "So, where are we going to dinner?" Nikolai asks conversationally, his accent stronger with the pain.

I hear sirens in the distance. No doubt someone called the cops when they heard the gunshot.

"What are you in the mood for?" I walk as swiftly as I can without drawing attention to us. The moment we're outside, I detach myself from Nikolai and go running for the Land Rover. Natasha is smart enough to keep walking as best she can, holding up Nikolai's weight.

As soon as I get to my Mercedes SUV, I jump in and start it up, backing out and straight down the aisle until Natasha and Nikolai get close in the rearview mirror.

I stop, hop out and throw open the door to the backseat. "Get in," I order Natasha.

She climbs in, and I help Nikolai, which is hard because he's starting to go limp.

"Fuck, fuck, fuck," I mutter as I finally manage to get him in. He doesn't stay upright on the seat, though. He spills over toward Natasha.

I yank my shirt off and ball it up. "Hold this to his wound," I bark. I roll Nikolai a little to check his back for blood.

"Okay, the bullet went through. That's good," I tell Nikolai. "Hold pressure on this side, too."

Natasha takes my shirt from me. "Do you have a first aid kit in here? With gauze? I need to pack the wound."

I shouldn't be surprised that Natasha would be capable in a pinch. Her mother's a homebirth midwife, and she's been unofficially assisting since she was a kid. I'm too angry to admire it now, though.

I reach under the front seat and pull out the med kit, opening it up. I toss the roll of gauze on the seat beside Nikolai.

"Pack it." I send her a narrowed gaze. "He dies, you die," I tell her flatly.

The color drains from her face, and she stares at me with wide frightened eyes. I register her fear as pain in my own body. A sick twist of my gut for being such a cocksucker to someone I care about. Threatening her life is unforgivable. Something we won't recover from.

But there is no *we*. That's what I have to remember.

There is no we now, nor can there ever be.

"Little harsh, no?" Nikolai mumbles right before I slam the door.

3

Natasha

He dies, you die.

Dima just threatened my life. *Dima*, the bratva bad boy I thought was the nicest of the guys in the Kremlin. I should have listened to my mom. She tried to tell me this. These men are dangerous, and they won't hesitate to kill anyone who threatens them.

I don't know how I could've thought there was potential between us.

I steal a glance at his twin Nikolai.

He raises his brows. "He's pissed," he says with exaggerated awe, like he's surprised, too. Like Dima never gets mad.

I rip open the package of gauze with trembling fingers while he holds the balled up shirt in place over his wound. Every part of me trembles—lips, chin, fingers, knees.

I'm not even sure what happened back there. *Alex shot Nikolai!* —that's what happened. I quickly unravel a length of gauze and use my teeth to rip it, then move Nikolai's hand and the combined bloody shirts—his and Dima's—to stuff the gauze in the wound the way I learned in my training to be an EMT. Before I realized it was too much trauma for me to stomach and set my sights on becoming a naturopath instead. I repeat the action for the exit wound.

I hear the ringing of a phone coming through the speakers. Dima's making a hands-free call through the car's system.

"*Da?*"

"Nikolai's shot," Dima clips. "He needs a doctor and blood. Type O positive. I can donate if you can't get any."

"Take him to the clinic—I'll get Blake to meet you there. What happened?" I recognize Ravil's terse voice. He's all-business.

In the rear-view mirror, I see a muscle in Dima's jaw tick. "Natasha brought a fucking Fed to the game."

A wave of ice cold washes over me, and my shaking increases five-fold. The parts of the puzzle my shocked brain hadn't been able to fit together suddenly snap into place.

Alex is a federal agent.

He used me to get to Nikolai.

God, I am such an idiot! How could I be so stupid?

"What?" Ravil asks in disbelief. "*Blayd'*. So what happened?"

"He was a rookie. Spoke Russian, that's probably why they put him on us. He panicked when he got made and took a pot-shot before we had a chance to disarm him. I told Oleg to leave him there for the Feds to deal with."

"Is he dead?"

"No. Knocked out."

"Why was Natasha at game?" Ravil asks, dropping the article.

Dima punches the dashboard, and I gasp at the crunch of hard plastic and the violence behind the gesture. "My fault. She asked and... I don't know. I couldn't say no because it was Natasha."

"*Blyad'*, Dima." Ravil sounds disgusted.

Because it was Natasha.

I flip that phrase over and over in my head, trying not to run too far with it. Part of me secretly rejoices. I was right—I do mean something to him! He couldn't refuse me the favor when I asked.

But then the twisting in the pit of my stomach tightens even more. Because that means the betrayal Dima feels over my actions must cut even deeper.

"Where is she now?"

"In the back seat with Nikolai."

"I see. I'll deal with her when I get there."

Another wash of cold floods through me. I nearly pee my pants like a frightened puppy.

"No, *I'll* deal with her," Dima snaps back.

I'm not sure what either of them means by *dealing with* me, but it can't be good.

It's probably really, really bad.

I just betrayed their organization and may have gotten Nikolai killed.

Dima probably meant it when he said if Nikolai dies, I die. Oh God, if they kill me, my mother will never survive the grief.

"Who is *pakhan* here?" The bark in Ravil's voice makes Dima stiffen.

"You are."

"Indeed. Now keep a cool head for Nikolai's sake. I will meet you there with help."

Dima purses his lips but doesn't answer. The call ends.

My next breath comes in on a silent sob—one of those terraced, hiccuping kinds.

"Shh," Nikolai says softly. "Everything will be fine." But his eyelids flutter closed.

"Wake up, wake up, wake up," I whisper urgently, not wanting Dima to hear.

I believe Dima now. My life depends on Nikolai not dying.

Nikolai's lashes flicker back open. "I won't die," he promises me. "It takes more than one cowardly bullet to put me down."

Tears stream down my face as Dima weaves through the Chicago streets. I sit sideways on the seat, my back and arms cramping from the awkward position I maintain to keep compression on Nikolai's wounds.

I try to catch Dima's gaze in the rear-view mirror. "I didn't know Alex was a Fed—I swear. I'm sorry."

"We'll discuss it later." He shuts me down.

I try not to think about all the bad things that could happen. To me. To Nikolai. To my mother. Will Ravil kick us out of the Kremlin? Will they shoot me and throw my body in Lake Michigan?

It takes about twenty minutes before Dima pulls into an alleyway and shuts the vehicle off.

He climbs out of the driver's seat and throws the back door open. When he sees Nikolai hasn't stirred, he lunges in and reaches for the pulse at his neck.

Nikolai's lids crack. "I'm not dead, asshole."

"Better not be," Dima mutters back. He scrubs a hand over his face, taking in the blood-soaked shirt and Nikolai's limp form.

"The bleeding has slowed," I tell him.

Dima smacks his forehead against the vehicle's door frame. "Get out." He beckons to me to come out his side.

I raise my brows in surprise. I thought I was supposed to be applying pressure.

"Now."

"Okay." I climb out, and his hands are instantly on me. His touch is quick and rough as his palms coast down my back, over the globes of my ass.

I sputter in surprise.

He follows the hem of my dress all the way around the skirt, and I finally realize what he's doing—checking for a wire. He thinks I'm working with the Feds, too. He puts his hands inside my dress and quickly checks my panties by brushing the backs of his knuckles over the front. He doesn't linger long enough to humiliate me, but that doesn't stop the hot flush from flooding my neck and chest, collecting in the hollow of my throat, creeping up my neck.

I try to shove him away, but he's immovable, still completing his check, sliding his fingers over the bodice of my dress. I'm not wearing a bra, and my stupid nipples get hard when he brushes across them.

He chokes a little on his breath. I try to hold in a whimper. He turns me around to check the back of the halter, and then he steps back. "Hand me your purse."

I grab my purse from the floor of the back seat and hurl it at him, blinking back the heat behind the bridge of my nose. He dumps it out on the floor of the Land Rover and sorts through it, obviously still searching for some kind of bug. He takes apart my phone and swiftly examines the insides. After he puts it back together, he does something with the settings, then pockets it rather than returning it to my purse. The rest of my things, he shoves back into my purse.

A car screeches in behind us, and a man I don't recognize jumps out. He ignores us and unlocks the door to the building and a half minute later jogs out with a spine board. "Are you Dima?" He rakes his gaze over Nikolai inside the Land Rover. I step back to make room for the board.

"Yeah," Dima says. "This is Nikolai. I'm a blood and organ match."

"I can see that." They are obviously identical twins. "All right, help me get him on the board."

Dima climbs in to take my place near Nikolai's shoulders, and the two men heft him onto the board, then carry him into the building. I run ahead to open the door, then follow.

Another car screeches into the alley and doors slam. Ravil and Maxim enter swiftly. Neither says a word to me as they pass, but Ravil's harsh gaze makes me shrink. I melt backward toward the door, and Ravil must sense it because he stops and turns.

"Come into the operating room, please, Natasha."

I note the *please*. He's still polite, even though his tone brooks no disobedience. But then, Ravil always did play at being refined. He hides his brotherhood tattoos under expensive dress shirts and slacks. His shoes are always shining. If not for the crude ink across his knuckles, you'd think he was born to rule a boardroom, not the Russian mob.

I follow the men into a fluorescent-lit operating room.

The building smells like antiseptic and animals, and I can hear the bark and whine of dogs down a hallway.

They put Nikolai on a stainless steel table, and the veterinarian removes the gauze. "Who packed the wounds?" he asks tersely.

"Natasha," Dima murmurs without looking at me. It's like he'd prefer to pretend I'm not here. I get it. He must think the absolute worst of me right now. Hell, so do I.

"Well done. Are you a medic?" the doctor asks me.

"I've been through EMT training."

"Can you put a needle in?"

I close my eyes and draw a steadying breath. I'm not trained in it, but I've seen my mother put in IV lines. "I can try."

I walk to Nikolai's side.

"No, in him." He jerks his head toward Dima. "I need his blood. The bags are in the lower right-hand cabinet over there." He shows me with his chin, as his fingers are busy putting an IV into Nikolai's hand.

I scurry to the cabinet and open it, dropping to my knees to find the bags. They're for animals, so smaller than human blood bags, but basically the same. I get the needle and tubing and put the set together.

Dima just stands there, his face as pale as his brother's as he looks on.

I find rubber gloves, the antiseptic, and a tube to tie around his arm.

"Okay, um, have a seat," I say to Dima.

He doesn't look at me as he pulls a chair out from the wall and sits in it. I crouch beside him, my tight cocktail dress making it all the more awkward, and I swab the area, then tie the rubber tube above his elbow.

I palpate his veins. Damn. Am I really going to do this? But the need to contribute somehow, to try to right my wrongs makes me push past my fear of screwing this up. I channel my mother's clean, efficient movements. Her calm in the face of anything. Deftly, I slip the large needle into his vein, open the port and let the blood flow in.

"That's good," the vet says when he looks over. "Put the bag down by his feet so gravity will make it fill."

I lay the blood bag on the floor and sit beside it, at Dima's feet, hugging my knees.

The room is quiet while the vet works on Nikolai. Vaguely, I hear him say he has to operate to repair a damaged portion of his colon.

35

When Dima's blood bag is full, I close the port and remove the needle.

"Get a new needle and put it into Nikolai's arm," the vet instructs me, somehow able to monitor my actions at the same time he operates.

I obey, even though I'm terrified I'm going to fuck it up. When I get the needle in, I hang the bag on the IV pole and release the port. "Um. Okay, I think I did it."

The doctor gives it a cursory glance, then refocuses on his work. "Good job. You're a big help, Natasha."

I make the mistake of sneaking a look at Dima and find his icy blue glower firmly resting on me.

A shiver runs through my body. Dima obviously doesn't agree.

And I can't decide what scares me more—anticipating what Ravil, the ruthless *mafiya* boss will do to me or the knowledge that I forever lost Dima's regard.

DIMA

Nikolai's wheezing makes my own gut burn with phantom pain. We've always been too close, he and I. Our lives are as intertwined as vines. The bratva has a rule—no family allowed. No wives, no children. Because we all become each other's brothers. But since Nikolai and I were already brothers, it was allowed. Nikolai had insisted we stayed as a team, and Igor allowed it.

But that was old-world bratva. Here, in the States, Ravil runs a more relaxed cell. He and Maxim both have wives. Oleg has a girlfriend. Families are allowed. Children, even. Ravil has a five-month-old in our penthouse compound.

I haven't felt this out of control since the night Alyona

told me the pancreatic cancer was untreatable. The level of adrenaline running through me has not sharpened my brain, it's only muddled it. There's a wild recklessness in me that could make me do something stupid.

I've already been too harsh with Natasha. I know she's scared, but I'm too pissed to fix it. Too terrified of losing Nikolai.

He *can't* die.

Especially not this way, when it's all my fault. I was thinking with my dick when I gave Natasha the location of the game. I knew it didn't make sense, but I couldn't tell her no. Now I could pay the ultimate price.

I stand a few feet from the table and watch Dr. Taylor, the veterinarian Ravil keeps on the payroll for this sort of situation, operate. The fact that he *has* to operate doesn't bode well for Nikolai. If he pulls through, he could have permanent side effects from this. Like a colostomy bag.

The fact that it's a veterinarian, not a trauma specialist, operating on my brother without the full range of resources that would be available in a human hospital makes me want to kill someone. But this is the life we chose. I got Nikolai into the bratva because of a girl. Now I may have ended his life because of a girl.

Blyad'.

But Dr. Taylor's good. I've seen him work before. He's a serious guy. He may be a vet, but he knows what he's doing. He doesn't seem to have any hang-ups or judgments about working for the Russian *mafya*.

There are never any questions. He just does the job and takes payment. I know he'll do his best.

"Is there—um, may I use a restroom?" Natasha asks. She's peeled off her rubber gloves and is staring at her blood-stained hands.

I jerk my head toward the reception area because I'm still not ready to talk to her, but Ravil shoots me a look.

He's afraid she's going to bolt.

I seriously doubt it, but you never know. My judgment is obviously totally impaired when it comes to the beautiful redhead. I also never contemplated the idea of her bringing a Fed to our game.

I follow her out and lean against the doorway when she goes into the bathroom. She catches sight of me when closes the door, and her startled gaze turns frightened. As angry as I am, it doesn't sit well with me. I've scared her beyond chastisement. Natasha wears the look of someone who believes terrible things are going to happen to her.

Well, no wonder. Did I actually threaten her life in the car? I didn't mean it. I would never harm a woman, especially not Natasha. Natasha is my constant torture. The woman I can't have but I can't make myself stop wanting.

Damn her for twisting me up like this! Flaying me alive. Making me fail my brother and my organization.

Fuck.

The toilet flushes and the sink turns on. And runs and runs.

Nyet. Suddenly the images of every action movie where the hero or heroine turns on the shower or sink and then crawls out the bathroom window flood my head. Was there a window in that bathroom?

I lurch for the bathroom door handle and wrench it open. Expecting it to be locked, I throw half my weight against the door… and tumble through when it flies inward.

Natasha screams. The water from her hands, which she was washing in the sink, splashes across me. "Jesus. What are you doing?" she snaps, the first sign of push-back she's given me, ever.

I step back, shaking my head. "I thought you'd left the water on and crawled out a window," I mutter.

Natasha scoffs and makes a show of looking around the tiny bathroom. "The invisible window?"

She's right. There's no window. A fact I would've known if I'd given any thought whatsoever to the location of the bathroom with regard to the layout of the building. My brain obviously is still not online.

"How long does it take to wash your hands?" I turn it back on her.

Her shoulders sag, and she looks at her hands, flipping them over to examine them. "Yeah, well, I was having a bit of a Lady Macbeth moment with the blood."

I don't know my English literature well enough to understand the reference, but I make a mental note to look it up the next time I'm in front of my computer.

Like any time I'm not behind a screen, I feel untethered; yet with tonight's events, it's hard to imagine going back there. I can't manipulate from behind the scenes tonight. Not when my brother's bleeding on a vet's table, and the woman I've vowed not to touch has forever shattered my sanctity. No code or hack can help Nikolai. There's no manipulation of fate I can orchestrate to change outcomes in our favor.

I back out of the bathroom to let her pass, but when she comes out, she steps into the mini-kitchen area next to the bathroom. Examining the Keurig, she asks, "Would you like a cup of coffee?"

"No," I say shortly then sigh. "Ravil probably will, though."

She snaps a fresh brew cup in, fills the machine with water, and places a mug underneath. When it fills, she makes a second cup, then walks past me into the reception area.

Damn her. I don't want her fucking sweetness, and the girl is pretty much always sweet. It changes nothing.

I follow her in and watch as she quietly offers the coffee to Ravil and Maxim, who both accept it from her. She ignores me and walks back, making another cup for herself and bringing little creamers and sugar in for Ravil and Maxim.

I settle against a wall and fold my arms across my chest, refusing to look at her, even though her silent presence fills the room.

Like Ravil told me when I was driving here. I need to keep a cool head—for Nikolai's sake. And that means keeping my fucking distance from Natasha, my own personal detonator.

4

Natasha

I really need a piece of chocolate. Or a whole barrel-full. My adrenals are tanking from the stress, and I'm shaky all over and running on empty.

"Natasha, we'll have a word with you now." Ravil tips his head toward the inner door of the lab.

Maxim follows him out.

For a moment, I can't move as ice-cold fear grips my throat, making it hard to breathe. Those dry sobs that hit me earlier in the vehicle return, and I stumble toward the door nearly hyperventilating.

Dima comes up to me from behind and catches my nape with a firm grip. "Hey."

I can't look at him. I know he hates me. Ravil hates me. I have no idea what they're going to do to me, but it can't be good.

"Hey," Dima repeats with more authority. "Look at me," he says in a low voice, meant only for my ears.

I work to calm my pulse as I meet his blue gaze.

Surprisingly, it's not as cold now—it seems more troubled than angry.

"Tell me now before we go in there—did you know?" he demands, brows down.

I shake my head, tears spearing my eyes. "I swear to God I didn't."

Dima searches my face for a moment then gives a nod. "If you're telling the truth, you'll be all right." His thumb lightly strokes over my pulse, sending tingles of awareness everywhere. "Ravil's not a monster. Just go in there and answer his questions honestly."

A ridiculous snort-sniff sound comes out of me as I try to stifle my sobs, and I turn away to hide my embarrassment.

He's being kind—I should be grateful. This is the Dima I thought I knew. But I can't get over the threat he made back in his car.

He dies—you die.

He meant it. I saw the threat in his icy gaze.

So I'm not sure I believe I'm going to walk out of this meeting safely.

Dima grasps my nape again and steers me down the hall. Ravil and Maxim are standing in the reception area of the veterinarian clinic. It's a pleasant reception area. The walls are painted a muted teal, the concrete floors are stained purple, and the furniture has modern simplicity.

"Have a seat." Ravil points to one of the chairs. As I settle into it, he turns a chair around backward and straddles it facing me, resting his forearms on the back. Dima and Maxim flank him with their chairs. The Spanish Inquisition.

Well, at least they don't have pliers out to pull off my fingernails. *Yet.* Still, I can't stop shivering.

It doesn't help that Ravil says nothing for a moment,

42

just considers me. Finally, he asks, "Why were you at my game?"

I will myself not to cry and draw a breath. "Alex wanted to go. He was my date." When Ravil says nothing, I stumble on. "I met him at the gym last month, and he asked me out. He's, um, Russian, also. Or half-Russian." I lick my lips, darting a glance at Maxim then back to Ravil. "We've been out a couple times—nothing serious." I resist changing my gaze to Dima when I say that part.

"When he found out where I lived, he seemed sort of excited. He'd heard of you guys. He knew Ravil's name, even."

No way, he'd gushed. *You live in the Kremlin? Do you know that's owned by the Russian mafiya?*

My face flames hot as I realize how I was played. How stupid I was. I thought he was genuinely interested in me, and I let myself get used.

"I don't know, he acted like he was sort of a fan-boy of the bratva. Like he wanted to join as a Russian heritage thing. He wanted an introduction. I wasn't super comfortable with that. Then he told me he heard you guys had a card game every Friday and asked if I could get him in. I wasn't sure about that, either, but I thought maybe I could go and bring him along."

Nothing shows on Ravil's face, but I sense his judgment of me. "And you told Dima all this when you asked to go?"

I swallow. Fuck.

This looks bad for me. Really bad.

"No," I choke. I scrape off the fingernail polish on my thumbnail with frantic movements. "I, um... he... I don't know why I didn't tell him about Alex."

Ravil cocks a brow like he doesn't believe me.

My stomach churns. I don't dare look at Dima, but I feel the weight of his glare.

When I don't say anything more, Ravil prompts, "That's not good enough, Natasha."

A tear escapes my right eye and slides down my cheek. I duck my head to hide it, switching my anxious scraping to the other thumbnail. "It just felt awkward, I guess."

"Awkward," Ravil echoes, doubt tinging his tone.

I don't want to explain the stupidity of it all. How I wanted Dima to ask me out. How talking about another guy wasn't going to help that lost cause. Ugh, and on some level, maybe I hoped showing up with a guy who was interested in me would make him jealous. Give him the push he needed.

But all of that seems trivial now. This wasn't about my dating life. It was about a federal agent infiltrating the bratva, and I abetted him. And in the process, Dima's twin got shot. Something he'll never forgive me for.

So yeah, the chances of him asking me out now or in the future are nil.

"I'm sorry," I croak, my voice scratchy with tears.

Ravil gives it another moment of excruciating silence before he says, "I am disappointed, Natasha. I consider you and your mother to be family. You were under my protection. This feels like a violation of trust."

I drag in a hiccuping sob and hold it, trying not to burst into tears. "I know." I bob my head. "I'm sorry," I repeat.

"You knew nothing about him being an FBI agent?"

"I swear I didn't. I had no idea. I realize now how stupid I was."

"What *do* you know about him?" Ravil asks.

I nibble my lip, trying to remember anything that might be helpful. "He went to Illinois State for college. I think he was a wrestler. He works at the gym where I take kickboxing."

"Where does he live?"

I try to think if he mentioned anything. "I-I don't know. Our dates were casual. No, um, hook-ups or anything." This time I do sneak a look in Dima's direction, but the anger I see on his face makes me quickly look away, the knot in my stomach growing tighter.

"What else can you tell us about him? When did he first start working at the gym? Has he been there all along?"

Oh, God. All the red flags were there. I rub my temples. "No, he just got the job about a month ago. He asked me out for coffee after class a few weeks ago. And then we had dinner last week." Why did confessing this make me want to hide under my chair?

Oh yeah, it was the glower coming from Dima's direction.

Ravil sends a glance in Dima's direction then blows out his breath. "Well, Natasha. I need you to make this right. You will go with Dima to the cabin to nurse Nikolai back to health. You'll stay there as long as it takes, no complaints."

I have no idea what "the cabin" is, but I nod, making myself agreeable. I'll have to cancel the few massage sessions I have booked, but it's not like I have any choice, here, is it?

Ravil's always played the part of the benevolent dictator to our community—the Russians living in his building. Our rent is low—probably one-quarter what it should be for such a beautiful building and highly-prized location. In return, we offer our loyalty. If the cops come asking questions, suddenly no one speaks English. When Ravil tells us no strangers are allowed in the building, we obey his rules and bend to his will.

My mother didn't want to accept his generosity

because she knew what he was, but she was drowning in debt from getting her Nurse Practitioner licensing to practice midwifery in the United States. She moved into the Kremlin for me—so I'd have a fighting chance at affording college—but she always cautioned me to keep my distance from the tattooed men who serve as our self-appointed protectors.

Ravil turns to look at Dima. "I'll let you sort the rest of it out with her in private as you see fit."

My stomach flip-flops as Dima turns an assessing gaze on me.

Does that mean he'll be punishing me somehow? In a way that requires *privacy*? I resist the urge to swallow, knowing he'll see it.

Dread mingles with something else. Something more...intriguing. A heat coils in my core now, thawing the ice that was clogging my veins.

"Yes," Dima agrees, his blue gaze on me stony and hard. "I will deal with her."

DIMA

I watch Natasha squirm under my stare. I hated when she shook and trembled over answering to Ravil, but I don't mind it so much now that I'm the one in charge of her.

Ravil just remanded her into my custody. Part of me wanted to refuse—I can hardly stand to look at her after the way she played me—but the thought of her having to answer to anyone else makes me want to punch the wall in.

If she's going to be punished for her sins, it will come from me.

Not that I'm the sadist in our bratva cell. That would

be Pavel, through and through. I suspect Ravil and Maxim also get a little kinky with their wives—and *Gospodi*, yes, I wish I didn't know that, but living in the same suite makes some dynamics a bit hard to hide.

I don't have big plans to torture Natasha. I'm still too pissed off to even speak to her at the moment, but having her managed by anyone else would only enrage me further.

"Is there anything else you need to tell me?" Ravil asks Natasha. "Anything you're keeping from me?"

Blyad'.

Based on the way she goes a little pale and starts scratching at her fingernail, I know there is something.

What now, my beautiful traitor?

"Um… I have a cat."

It takes me a moment to assimilate her words, and I have to ignore the way my heart flip-flops in my chest.

She has a cat. That's her last big secret.

There is no way this girl is a mole. She's far too innocent. She's not working with the Feds. She got played by a guy and then played me to make him happy. I fight the urge to forgive her for everything.

She rushes on, "I know we're not allowed to have pets in the building, but I found him abandoned as a kitten, and he needed nursing back to health, and then… I just couldn't let him go."

Gospodi, she's adorable. I rub my face to hide my fascination with her. This is why I find this girl intoxicating. Addictive. She's so youthful—pure and precious. Undamaged. A bright light in a world with so few bright lights.

Ravil's lips twitch. "I already knew about your unsanctioned pet."

"You did?"

He touches his fingertips together. "Very little happens in my building that I don't know about, Natasha."

Thanks to my cyberstalking, of course.

He sits back. "I will have someone stop in and feed your furry friend while you are at the cabin and your mother is in Russia."

She ducks her head. "Thank you."

"Go back and see if Dr. Taylor requires your assistance."

She stands, her high heels making her slender legs appear even longer than usual. I loathe the revealing dress she's wearing. That she wore it for him. In my irrational and over-emotional state, it seems like Nikolai got shot because she put that fucking dress on for Alex.

Ravil waits until the door to the clinic shuts then asks, "What do you think?"

"I'm inclined to believe her," Maxim says.

I scrub my hand across my face. "Me too, but my judgment is shit when it comes to her."

"Obviously," Maxim says drily.

"Svetlana's in Russia now? The timing of that is suspicious," Maxim muses.

Svetlana is Natasha's mother, the proud and stubborn midwife who delivered Ravil's baby, Benjamin.

"Right. She could've gotten her mother out of harm's way before taking this risk." Ravil looks at me. "Look into it. See if you can find out exactly where she is now and what she's doing."

"I left my computer in the hotel room."

"Adrian or Oleg would've taken it. I'll have someone drive out to the cabin tomorrow with food and supplies," Ravil says.

"Thank you," I mutter.

Ravil's eyes narrow as he considers me. "Are you going to tell me if you find anything after you investigate her?"

He's asking whether I'll protect Natasha from him if it comes down to it.

I hesitate. Would I protect her? Fuck yes. The instinct is there. Even as angry as I am with her, I'd still take a bullet for that girl in a heartbeat. But would I hold back information from my *pakhan* for her?

No. Ravil is the fairest man I know. If Natasha's trouble for us, I trust him better than I trust myself to handle things.

I nod. "Yeah." I scrub a hand over my face. "I'm sorry about the car—"

"We're good," Ravil interrupts. "I understand she's your soft spot."

"More like my fucking Kryptonite," I mutter. Because Natasha single-handedly wreaked me tonight, and I'm usually the one who's thought of and prepared for everything. I lost all reason when she looked at me with those sea-green eyes and asked for a favor that made no sense.

The door from the clinic opens, and Dr. Taylor comes out, Natasha trailing behind. "I'm finished. I repaired the colon and put a drain in. He's on a drip of painkillers and antibiotics. Moving him isn't advised, but you obviously can't keep him here." He addresses Ravil but includes me in his eye contact. "Natasha knows how to administer the drip and adjust the drain. I've packed up the supplies you'll need. I'd like daily updates and am willing to do a home visit in the next forty-eight hours to check on his progress if that's… agreeable."

"Video or teleconferencing would be preferred," Ravil answers smoothly. Showing an outsider the location of the cabin would defeat the point of having the cabin. Of course, Natasha would know now, unless I make her cover her head with a hood, an idea that turns my stomach.

Dr. Taylor nods. "That's fine. Let's video tomorrow, so

I can take a look at everything. I'll send you with a pressure cuff as well." He glances at Natasha. "You know how to use it, I assume?"

She nods.

"Let's carry him out," Ravil says. We use the body-board, and I put one of the back seats forward to lay Nikolai down flat like I'm transporting lumber. Natasha crawls in the remaining backseat, positioned near his head.

"Keep him comfortable," I growl, throwing her a dark look before I slam the door.

The order is totally unnecessary. I know without a shadow of a doubt that Natasha will take care of him. That's her personality. That's why she made herself indispensable to the vet, brought coffee out to Ravil, and learned everything she would need to know to act as Nikolai's nurse.

Still, I'm not going to soften my heart toward her again.

I can't. Not when the consequences are this terrible.

Natasha

I JERK awake from what must've been a dream although it exactly represented my present moment. As in, I dreamed I was in the Land Rover, sitting beside Nikolai, trying to keep his head stabilized on a turn.

The vehicle bumps and jostles, and I realize it was the change to a dirt road that woke me. By the glowing clock on the dash, it's nearly four in the morning. Dima drives another ten minutes or so then parks the Land Rover in the dark. I blink, my eyes getting used to the darkness.

Dima gets out without a word and slams the door. He walks toward the darkened building.

A few moments later, a light comes on, illuminating a large, wooden wraparound porch. Lights go on inside the cabin, giving its windows a warm yellow glow. I'm not sure you can really call it a cabin. Yes, it's made of logs, but it's huge and looks newly constructed and expensive.

"We're here," I say softly to Nikolai, even though he seems to be out cold. The doctor said the pain meds should keep him asleep until morning.

I climb out and open the back gate of the Land Rover and slide the board toward me.

"You take that end." Dima appears behind me.

I swallow. This could be tough with just the two of us, but I can do it. At least I have his lighter half. "'Kay." I grip the board and back up.

Dima slides in to take the other side and then walks backward up the steps and through the door, which he propped open. I follow his lead into a giant living room area with vaulted ceilings. He leads me to what appears to be a master bedroom, with a giant king bed that he's already pulled the covers down on.

I'm starting to grunt with the weight, and Dima must notice because he moves quickly, sliding the board onto the bed and taking over my portion until the entire thing is supported. Then he stares down at his brother.

"Should we try to slide him off it?" I ask.

"I don't know." The weariness and defeat in Dima's voice make me want to drop to my knees and howl for what's happened to his beloved brother.

I have to fix this. To fix Nikolai. I crawl up on the bed beside him on my knees. "You steady him, and I'll see if I can just slip this out without jostling him too much."

"Slip it out. Right. Good luck with that," Dima

mutters, but he slides his two palms under Nikolai, one under his hips, the other under his mid-back. "Go."

I tug. It doesn't move. Dammit. I lean all my weight backward, and it slides a little in a jerk. I gasp, but Nikolai's body remains relatively undisturbed. I yank again with all my weight, and the board slides out. "Got it," I say needlessly.

I think I must want him to praise me or thank me or just somehow acknowledge me, but he doesn't. He just stares down at his brother stonily.

"Pick a bedroom upstairs. I'll stay with Nikolai." Once more, I hear how weary he is, and I feel stupid for wanting anything from him. Of course, he has nothing to give. And all of this is my fault.

I kick off my high heels—the ones I'm about ready to throw into a deep lake because my feet ache so badly—and pick them up to walk up the stairs.

I don't want to go to bed—not before things have been straightened out between Dima and I. I want to somehow make things right.

But I'm too tired to think straight, and he's obviously too angry to listen.

Tomorrow, I will fix things.

I hope.

5

Dima

I'm driving over an icy bridge. Alyona is beside me, chattering about friends of ours. About the concert we're going to see that weekend. Visibility is shit because it's snowing, and I don't see the brake lights in front of me until it's too late. I slam on the brakes, which sends us into a tailspin. We crash through the guardrail and hurtle over the edge into the icy river. Alyona screams and screams, but she's Natasha now. Natasha, covered in Nikolai's blood, a look of horror on her face. And then I realize Nikolai's lying unconscious in the back. He's been shot, and we won't be able to save him because we're crashing through the ice. Water seeps in through the windows as the car sinks. It's not my car, it's Ravil's—he's going to be so pissed I totaled it.

"What the fuck have you done?" Nikolai demands, waking and sitting up. He's looking at me, but the gun he points is at Natasha.

I turn and punch him in the face. "Leave her alone. It's not her fault—it's mine."

Fuck.

I wake, cold with sweat and shock. I find Nikolai beside me in the darkness and move my face in close to listen for his breath.

Still alive.

Thank God.

He's alive, and we're at the cabin. I've only slept a couple of hours.

My dreams were a knotted mess of trauma and guilt. Too much to even begin to climb out of. I consider getting up—dawn is just starting to break—but I'm not willing to leave Nikolai's side.

As if me lying beside him will make any kind of difference.

It won't for him.

"*Posti, brat,*" I murmur in the darkness. *I'm sorry, brother.*

Natasha

I wake with an aching head and terrible breath and guilt that adds an extra fifty pounds to my chest. I slept in my stupid cocktail dress, which now feels like another punishment.

Last night, a million years ago, when I put it on, I felt so seductive. I'd been thinking about impressing Dima, remembering his erections every time I massaged him. Hoping he might see me as worthy of asking out, especially now that there was competition.

Now I wish to God I'd gone in a pair of yoga pants and a tank top. At least they would've made better pajamas. I can't stand to be in this thing for another second. To say I'm not the cocktail dress type would be an understatement. I live in skinny jeans and Chucks.

I search the drawers in the bedroom I'm in for a t-shirt but find nothing but a spare set of sheets and pillowcases for the bed.

I don't hear any sounds from downstairs, and part of me just wants to keep hiding up here. I don't want to face Dima and his wrath and whatever punishment he has planned for me while I'm locked up here with him.

But I need to be a big girl. Still, I slip down the stairs as silently as possible. If Dima's asleep, I'll let him stay that way. I peek in the open bedroom door and find him lying on top of the bed beside Nikolai, asleep. I guess I wasn't the only one who slept in their clothes last night.

I take a look around. Last night it was dark, and my brain wasn't working. Today, I'm stunned by how beautiful the cabin is. It's more like a forest mansion, really. A great room with vaulted ceilings has wall-to-wall windows along one side with a spectacular view of the forest. Leather furniture is organized around the view and the fireplace on one end of the great room. On the other, a long farm table anchors the open-concept dining area, which is beside the large, well-appointed kitchen.

As I discovered last night, the curving staircase leads to an upper-level wraparound hallway, with banisters over-looking the great room. There are four bedrooms and two bathrooms up there.

I head into the kitchen, starting a pot of coffee as quietly as possible. The refrigerator is empty except for condiments, but there's some food in the pantry. Canned goods. A pancake mix that only requires water. A half a bag of chocolate chips.

I definitely need chocolate today. I pop a few chips in my mouth and go about making chocolate chip pancakes. I'm a firm believer in adding chocolate to everything, espe-cially when I'm stressed.

Dima still hasn't woken by the time I finish, so I eat a couple, lamenting the lack of butter, but finding real maple syrup to drizzle over them instead.

Then I finally stop stalling and go into Nikolai's room. I need to give him his meds through a new drip although I can't remember if we even brought the supplies in from the Land Rover last night. I do a cursory check of the room but don't find them.

Outside, I find the Land Rover open, and I carry the cardboard box of supplies inside, setting them gently on the dresser beside a pistol and Dima's glasses.

I didn't know Dima had a gun. I've seen them on Ravil and Maxim before but never on Dima.

I stare at it for a moment.

"You touch that pistol, Natasha, and the gloves come off."

I whirl, anger surging like bile. Dima's sitting up in the bed, his blond hair rumpled, his face no less beautiful when he's being cruel. He pats the bedside table without taking his gaze off me and I realize he's looking for his glasses.

I hand them to him. "Seriously, Dima? What in the hell do you think I'm going to do with it? Shoot you? Make you give me the keys, so I can run away?" I throw my hands in the air with exasperation. "I *live in your building.* My *mother* lives in your building. I know this is my fault, but I'm in this with you. I'm not the enemy."

Dima swings his long legs off the bed and stalks past me and out of the room without answering.

Great. So I'm getting the silent treatment now. Peachy.

Nikolai groans. "Well, good-fucking-morning to you, too."

"Nikolai!" I gasp, moving to his side. "I'm sorry. You're probably in pain. You were supposed to get your meds a couple hours ago."

"That explains it," he says weakly.

"Just give me a minute. It's intravenous, so it will work quickly."

I swiftly attach the IV bag and the painkiller to the tube still in the back of his hand and unlock the port, as the veterinarian showed me. My hands shake nearly as badly as they did last night, just from that little interaction with Dima, and I have to work to steady my breath.

"You've got my brother all kinds of grouchy," Nikolai observes.

"Tell me about it," I mutter as I work. "And I thought you two were the laid-back ones."

"We are. We were. Not with you around, though."

I wince. Finishing with the IV, I take his temperature and write it down, as Dr. Taylor requested.

"You know what I think?" Nikolai's accent is thick. He sounds a little drunk from pain.

"What?"

"Dima is madder about you bringing a date to the game than about me getting shot."

For a moment, my heart stops. Then it trips up to a gallop. "I-I'm sure that's not true," I say, trying to sound casual while I'm reeling.

Another confirmation that I was right. Dima's into me. Judging by what Nikolai's saying, he's *way* into me.

So... WTF? Why has this guy never acted on it? Why won't he ask me out? Why won't he make a move?

I attach a pressure cuff to Nikolai's arm and check his blood pressure, writing it down on the sheet of paper as well. "I'm sorry you got shot," I murmur as I work. "I would do anything for a redo on last night. I'm just so sorry."

"I forgive you," he says magnanimously. "It's Dima you need to work on."

I look toward the open door, but I don't know where he's gone. Now that Nikolai's let me in on his secret—that he is interested in me… that knowledge fuels me, gives me the courage to find him and try to explain myself.

He deserves the truth.

Dima

I stand in Ravil's office, surveying computer equipment that I set up here, trying to figure out if I have what I need to start a full-scale investigation into Alex.

"Dima?"

Blyad'. I can't get away from her.

I turn to find Natasha standing in the doorway. She's still in that fucking dress. The one that shows every single curve of her lithe body. It makes her look like a grown-up, someone I could do all the dirty things I frequently imagine doing to her.

"Get out." I seriously cannot deal with her. I'm not ready. I need more information. I need to get behind a fucking computer!

She doesn't listen, though. She comes in, drifting ever closer, close enough for me to catch her ginger-peach scent. The one that seems to match the red glints in her coppery hair.

"I'm sick over what I did. What a mess I made of things. I… um… I've been trying to figure out why I wasn't upfront about bringing Alex to the game."

I grind my molars and finally lift my icy gaze to hers. I even go so far as to take a few menacing steps in her direction.

She registers the threat, backing up toward the wall. I want to kick my own ass for scaring her, but pushing her

away—keeping myself shut off from her allure—is impera-
tive. I can't let myself soften toward her. She's already the
hugest liability possible.

"Honestly?" Her fingers tangle together at her waist;
she's doing that fidgety thing she does when she's nervous.
"I think I was trying to get a rise out of you."

My brain scrambles in disbelief.

Natasha is not the manipulative type. At least, I didn't
think so. She's sweet and honest and giving.

"I hoped you'd be jealous and finally make a move."

I'm suffocating suddenly by the friction of her words
ricocheting inside my body. She hoped I'd...be jealous. And
make a fucking move.

I close the distance between us, my hand grasping her
throat as I push her up against the wall. Her green eyes
widen, but I don't have time to watch them dilate because
my mouth crashes down on hers, taking everything I've
wanted all these torturous months. It's a brutal kiss.
Punishment for all the agony she's put me through. For
what she's still doing to me.

I lick between her lips to lash her with my tongue. I let
my teeth scrape her lips, I suck her tongue into my mouth.
She gives it back with passion. So much more eagerness
than I expect or deserve.

Well, hell. My cock swells against my zipper. My kiss
grows more feral.

She reaches for my dick, giving the hardened outline
against my jeans a squeeze. I catch her wrist and spin her
to face the wall, punishing her with a sharp smack to
her ass.

She holds still like she's waiting for more.

I hesitate. This is where I should pull back. Shove her
out of the room and slam the door. But there was a certain
satisfaction that came with slapping her ass. A release of

the pent-up lust, frustration, and anger that had me ready to explode.

She certainly deserves a spanking after what she did.

I deserve this release.

I flatten both her palms against the wall and pin them with my left hand as I get busy slapping her ass with my right.

She gasps, squeezing her butt, but doesn't break position. She likes it.

Godammit.

I rub the bulge of my cock against one of her buttcheeks as I squeeze and knead the other one roughly.

Her moan is one hundred percent female pleasure. I yank the hem of her dress up above her waist, furious when I see the little g-string tucked between her cheeks.

"Did you wear this for him?" I snarl, hooking my finger under the string and pulling up to cinch the fabric against her clit.

"No!" she gasped. "I wore it so I wouldn't have panty lines with the dress, that's all," she rushes to explain. "And I wore the dress for you." The second part is softer, and it slips in below my defenses, reaching down my throat to grip my heart and yank on it.

I slap her bare ass, watching my handprints bloom, needing the distraction from the effect of her words.

"I'm not yours to tempt," I snarl, spanking harder than I mean to. I don't want her dressing for me. I didn't ask for that. I can't fucking withstand my desire if she does that.

She yelps at the intensity, and I stop to rub. I step in close, needing more contact than just my hand on her ass. I grind my dick against her hip and slip one hand down her panties in the front and continue to knead her heated ass with the other. She keeps her hands against the wall like a good girl.

The catch of her breath hangs tender and raw between us. My finger parts her folds, and I find she's dripping wet. Slick with arousal—as turned on as I am.

There's no stopping now. Giving her a spanking without getting her off would be a form of abuse, and I'm not that guy.

So even though I shouldn't, even though I've vowed never to take another woman, I curl my fingers, molding my palm around her mons and slipping my index and middle fingers into her welcoming channel.

"Dima," she moans, like the temptress. A siren luring me to my demise.

She feels as sweet as I know her to be. I grind the heel of my hand over her clit as I deliver another spank to her backside.

"Dima." The way she says my name will be my undoing. I'll hear that needy, desperate rasp in my ears echoing when I try to sleep, when I shower, when I fucking breathe, until the day I die. I slide my middle finger under the g-string in the back to find her anus, pressing there at the same time I work her clit in front.

"Dima!" There's shock in her voice, and her hips buck under my hands.

I work her from both sides, working my fingertip into her back hole as she undulates her hips to take my fingers deeper into her tight channel.

"I...I..." She comes all over my fingers, her muscles squeezing and releasing, her pelvic floor lifting, her anus tightening. "Oh my God!"

I close my lips against the string of praises I want to shower her with. Not that she doesn't deserve them all. I have never in my life seen anything so spectacular as Natasha coming. But Natasha is not my lover. Not my girlfriend. Not my anything. To keep things from turning intimate, I remove my fingers the moment she's done.

Almost as if she anticipated my hasty departure, she whirls the moment I do, reaching once more for my aching cock, heavy in my jeans.

"No." I catch her wrist, but she's already on her way down to her knees, and I suddenly stop, arrested by the sight.

By the idea.

She wants to suck me off.

I can't let her. I definitely shouldn't. But she's already unbuttoning my pants, freeing my very painful erection.

And fuck, I've been hard for this girl since the moment I first met her.

I need this.

If I don't let her do it, I won't be able to stop thinking about it. It will cause me to make more stupid decisions when it comes to her.

Yes, I should just let her do her thing. Work this out of my system, so I can finally release it and let it go.

She fists my cock and licks around the head, teasing my skin with her tongue. A shudder of pleasure makes me sway on my feet. I need to gather her hair away from her face, so I can watch, so I can see the incredible spectacle of those pouty pink lips wrapped around my throbbing member. She lifts her gaze to my face as she sucks hard, sliding the head of my cock into the pocket of her cheek. I wrap her hair around my fist in the back and use it to guide her over my cock. She turns her head one way and the other, driving me wild.

"Fuck." I'm already about to come. It's been forever since I've had a girl's mouth on me. Since I've fucked anything but my own fist. And dammit, for the last year, every time I have, it's been with the image of her beautiful face in my mind. "*Malysh.*" I didn't mean to let the endearment slip from my lips, but how could I not croon *baby* when she's treating me like a fucking king? When she's massaging my balls, then further back, seeking my prostate gland.

That undoes me. Remembering every excruciating massage I suffered through, imagining exactly this. How expert her small hands are at finding all the places I want them. How they're magic now, tugging at my cock, making it long and thick on her tongue.

I shout, my balls drawing up tight, my thighs starting to quake. "*Bozhe moi!*" I shout, losing control. I hold her head in place and push in and out of her mouth, then pull out just before I come, intending to spill over my fist. She pulls my hips back, though, sticking her tongue out to catch my essence.

I can only stare in utter shock. Sweet, angelic Natasha with the friendly girl-next-door vibe just sucked my dick like a porn star. Knowing she's had practice—quite a bit of it—makes me want to wring the necks of every guy she's ever touched. Especially Alex—even though she swore she hasn't had sex with him.

"*Gospodi*, Natasha." My awed croak makes her lift her big green eyes to my face. Rather than well-deserved confidence beaming from her face, what I see is far more crippling to my already detonated will-power—naked adoration. She's looking up at me like she thinks *belongs* on her knees at my feet, giving me the best blowjob of my life. Like worshipping my cock was a gift to her, not a punishment.

The guilt that soaks through me is crippling. Not just for my betrayal of Alyona's memory but for toying with Natasha. She doesn't deserve this.

I shove my cock back in my jeans and zip them, taking

a step back. "Fuck. I shouldn't have——" I break off, shaking my head. "I didn't mean to do that." I back toward the door, unable to avert my gaze from the disaster I made, based on the horrified expression on Natasha's face. "I'm sorry, it was a mistake."

6

Natasha

What. The actual. Fuck?

I hear the front door close and then the Land Rover start up. Seriously? Dima's literally running away right now?

My face burns as I find my way to my feet and rearrange the stupid cocktail dress back down my hips. My ass tingles and smarts from Dima palm, and that part still makes my tummy flip flop with excitement.

I've never orgasmed from being fingered before, and that was singularly the most erotic sexual experience I've ever had. Not that I have all that much sexual experience —I still live with my mom, after all.

I stand there, stunned, rewinding and reviewing our encounter. He thought it was a mistake.

Why?

What about getting some obviously much-needed sexual relief from me could be a mistake. Unless...

There was someone else.

But how could there be? I've never seen him with a

woman. He rooms alone in the penthouse suite. Did he leave a woman back in Russia? Maybe he can't go back because he's wanted there.

It would explain why he treats me like a wicked temptation—something he wants but can't have. Someone he borderline-resents for attracting him.

I'm not yours to tempt.

For some reason, the thin gold band he wears on his pinky finger floats up in my mind, and my stomach twists. Call it women's intuition. A gut instinct—whatever.

I suddenly know that it was given to him by her. Whomever she is.

And I hate her for being the one who holds his heart.

Anger toward Dima bubbles up, and I stomp into the kitchen to clean up the pancakes. I throw the ones I'd saved for Dima into the trash. He can damn well fend for himself. Going into an angry cleaning frenzy, I scrub the kitchen until it's spotless, not that it wasn't clean before I cooked breakfast.

Then I head upstairs and take a shower.

Of course, I still don't have any clothes to change into, a fact that is really starting to irritate me. Why couldn't I get stuck in a cabin in a pair of yoga pants and a comfy t-shirt? Why did it have to be a body-hugging cocktail dress that restricts my movements and breathing?

I put the damn thing back on and stomp downstairs. I'm really out of temper now.

I'm usually the pleaser in any group—the one trying to make sure everyone's comfortable and happy, but after being humiliated by Dima, anger is my go-to. It's either that or cry, and I'm not going to give him that satisfaction.

I check on Nikolai again. He'd been sleeping when I finished cleaning the kitchen, but he's awake now.

I bring him a glass of water with a straw and hold it to his mouth, so he can sip.

"Are you hungry at all? The doctor said you could have broth or juice today and soft foods starting tomorrow."

"*Nyet.*"

"Okay, tell me when you are. Should I bring a television in here or something?"

"Nah. I'm going to sleep some more. After you tell me what happened."

"Pardon me?" I pick up the pressure cuff and arrange it around his arm, watching the dial

"What did Dima do?"

I hate that my face gets hot. It's impossible for a redhead to hide a blush. "Nothing," I snap, the memory of what we'd done turning my core molten again. I shove the erotic thoughts away and bury them under my anger. "He left. I don't know where he went." I write the blood pressure down on the piece of paper the vet gave me then take Nikolai's temperature.

"Was he a *mudak*?" Nikolai asks as I beam the scanner at his forehead.

"Yeah," I breathe. "Total dick." His temperature isn't elevated, so I don't write it down. I turn away from Nikolai, fidgeting with the equipment.

I could ask Nikolai about the other woman. About the ring.

"Um… does Dima have a girlfriend?"

"No. Definitely not."

Huh. I turn. "Why definitely not?"

Nikolai closes his lids, his head falling back on the pillow. "That's Dima's story to tell," he says.

Gah. "So he *is* unavailable?"

Nikolai's gaze is musing. "Is that what he told you?"

"More or less."

Nikolai shakes his head. "Fucker."

"You didn't answer my question." I'm not usually bold or pushy, but I feel like I'm hanging onto my sanity by a string here. I have to fight to regain some equilibrium.

"I guess he thinks he is," Nikolai mumbles. His lids are drifting closed.

I sigh and watch him as he drifts into sleep. And then I have no idea what to do with myself. I go over to make up the other side of the bed—where Dima slept.

Like an idiot, I lower my face to his pillow and breathe in his clean masculine scent.

Nikolai doesn't stir. Seeing him there, so pale, his clothes cut away for the surgery, the remaining tatters still a crusty, bloody mess, his hands swollen with fluid retention from the IV, I'm shaken by another wave of guilt. Of fear.

What if Nikolai dies? If I'm responsible for costing Dima the one person he loves most in the world? I hate that I was so gullible. That Alex used me to do this.

I crawl into the bed beside Nikolai and pick up his hand without the IV in it. Using the very light touch used for lymphatic drainage, I start to massage out the fluid, up his arm and in the direction of his heart. It may not be much, but I can do this one thing for him. Maybe it will help.

DIMA

When I'm in the Land Rover, I plug Natasha's dead phone into the charger. I disabled tracking on it back at the vet's place last night, but I'm pissed at myself for not looking at it sooner. If my head were in the game, I wouldn't have gone to bed last night without reading every message she has on there and thoroughly investigating every source of information I could get from it.

The trip to the closest store takes twenty-five minutes. It's a gas station/convenience store for hikers and campers, so it features some random shit like mosquito repellent, hats, and t-shirts. I get milk, eggs, bread, and other basics, then grab a few of the t-shirts. I'm still in my undershirt, which is stained with Nikolai's blood. When the clerk stares at it, I look down and grimace. "Hunting accident," I tell him.

When I get back in the vehicle, the phone has charged enough to come on, and I check her calls and texts.

One text from Alex at six this morning, one phone call an hour ago. The text is simple, it just says, *Are you all right?*

I listen to the voicemail. "Natasha, I need to know if you're all right. *Fuck!* Please let me know as soon as possible."

Mudak. I want to cut off his balls and shove them down his throat.

I text back the single word, *yes.*

I doubt he'll be dumb enough to accept that since it could easily—and did—come from someone else, but no response might make the asshole itchier.

Then I realize I might be able to get more out of him, and I add *No thanks to you.*

I don't know what the fuck we're going to do about him. About the Feds. Or a better question might be, what they plan to do about us. I had a camera running in that hotel room, so everything was recorded. If Alex claims it was self-defense and Nikolai pulled a gun first, I can prove him wrong.

But my gut says he was as derailed by what happened last night as we were. The kid is young, and he made a split-second decision that ultimately was a bad judgment call. I don't think he knew what he was doing. I don't know —there was something sort of off-the-books about the whole thing.

I drive back to the cabin. As I pull up and get out, a sickening thought occurs to me. Natasha could've tried to run. She didn't have a vehicle, but she could've been ballsy or desperate enough to try to hike out of here to find another cabin or hitchhike on the main forest road.

I didn't think about it when I left because it's fucking Natasha, and she's blinded me again with my desire for her. I would say it's not like her to get feisty and run—she accepted Ravil's edict that she come here to nurse Nikolai with total grace—but if she has, I know whose fault it is.

Mine.

I'm the one who's been a total bastard to her.

I forget the groceries and sprint for the door, throwing it open and stalking inside. I quickly scan the living room with a sweeping gaze. No sound in the kitchen. I jog to Nikolai's room, and then I freeze, my heart choking my throat for a different reason.

Natasha is *in bed with my twin.*

Holding his hand.

"What the fuck are you doing?"

The serenity on her face instantly evaporates, and I hate myself for making her glare. "I'm working this fluid retention out of his arm. What's your problem?"

I shake my head, backing up. "Nothing," I mutter. "No problem."

My chest constricts. She's working the fluid retention out of his arm. Of course she is. Natasha is a healer— that's what she does. She's nothing but kindness and generosity.

I'm the prick who makes her suck my dick and then bails.

But no.

She might not be so innocent. I need to abandon all my own personal opinions of her and dig into data. Data doesn't lie.

Swallowing hard, I go back out to the Land Rover and bring in the groceries. As I put them away, Natasha comes into the kitchen.

"I can do that," she says in a low voice.

I turn to look at her but don't answer. I don't want to accept her sweetness. On one hand, this is punishment. She's here to serve, to make up for the incident she played a part in causing. But I can't stand to receive her help. Because I know if I do, I'll want more.

So fucking much more.

I'll want everything.

And I can't do that.

I continue putting things away, and she joins me without an invitation.

"Nikolai woke up for a little while. He didn't want any broth or juice." The vet said Nikolai's IV has electrolytes and nutrients in it, in addition to his meds, so I'm not worried about him not being hungry.

I still don't answer. I hate her for trying to make conversation. I hate myself for being such an asshole.

"This shirt is for you. They didn't have any shorts or pants." I toss the smallest t-shirt in her direction. "There's a toothbrush and toothpaste, too. And a comb. Do you use a comb?" *Gospodi*, why does it feel so intimate to ask her about her hair care? It's not like we're moving in together. She's my fucking prisoner.

She holds up the basic white shirt which has a boat on it and the words, *I'd rather be fishing.* "Wow. This will look great on me. Thanks," she quips drily.

I try not to look her way because if I do, I'm going to

be examining—for the umpteenth time—how hot she looks in that curve-hugging dress she's been wearing for the past eighteen hours. The one I peeled up her hips a few hours ago. The one she said she wore for me.

She's a goddamn torture to me in it. Hopefully the ugly shirt will remedy it.

"Do you still have my phone?"

"Yes." I don't look her way. I heat a frying pan to cook a few eggs. I wasn't hungry this morning, but now I'm even crankier than when I left.

"May I have it?" She walks close to me—way too close—and holds out her hand.

I don't look her way. "No." I drop some butter in the pan.

I hear her little intake of breath. The ripple of shock that goes through her. "Why not?" she demands. There's a note of defensiveness there.

"Because I need to search it. And yes, your *date* has called and texted to make sure you're all right." I crack three eggs and drop them into the butter then salt the hell out of them.

I expect a reaction about the date thing, but I don't get one. Instead, she puts her hands on her hips and considers me. "When you're done searching, may I have it?"

I hesitate, then remember my fears of her running. "No."

She draws in a measured breath like she's trying to keep her temper. I've never seen her mad, and for some reason, the idea gets me hard. What is it that's hot about an angry woman? Just that flare of passion that men imagine can be changed to sexual charge? Or is the desire to tame her—to take control? To master her and make her beg?

"Why not? Do you think I'd call someone for help? Do

you think I'd try to run? Where would I even go? I live in your building—it's not like I could hide."

"And your mother is conveniently out of the country at the moment."

Her gasp of shock couldn't be faked. But then, I don't trust my judgement when it comes to her. She pulls a spatula from the drying rack. For one second, I think she plans to use it as a weapon against me, but she angles it toward my eggs and lifts her chin.

Aw fuck. She's looking out for my eggs, which are getting crispy around the edges. I *hate* how considerate she is. It makes it so damn hard to fight the part of me that wants all in with her. I flip the eggs and reach for a plate.

"Really, Dima?" The hurt on her face appears genuine as well. "I would think you know me better than that. My mother and I do as Ravil bids. We turned a blind eye when he kept Lucy there against her will. Pretended we didn't speak English. I gave her massages, and my mother provided her medical care. We treated Oleg's bullet wound without asking any questions. I would think you would trust us by now."

"It was my trust in you that got us into this, wasn't it?"

She turns away. "I didn't know he was a Fed, and I wasn't a party to his infiltration plan." Her voice is quiet but stubborn.

I should tell her I believe her. Because I'm mostly sure I do.

But again, I can't trust my judgment. I need to look at the data. Follow trails. I need to be sitting behind a screen —the only place I know how to live.

"So I'm a prisoner here." It's a statement, not a question.

I walk past her to sit at the long rustic farm table to eat my eggs. "Maybe think of it more as detention. You're

73

here as a consequence. We're still examining the finer points of what happened."

"You do that." She picks up the t-shirt and toiletries and walks out in her bare feet. "You won't find anything on me."

I crane my neck to watch her climb the stairs.

I sure as hell hope she's right.

7

Natasha

I go upstairs to my room, but the crunch of car tires on the dirt drive outside sends me to the window.

I watch as Maxim, Oleg, the giant bratva enforcer, and Story, his musician girlfriend, climb out of an SUV. Story's hair has changed color since I saw her last week. Instead of all platinum, her bob is now accented with two bold chunks of a beautiful magenta in the front.

Oleg brings a cooler in with him, and Maxim carries a plastic crate filled with what looks like wires and cords or other electronic equipment.

I hear the door open and shut, and Dima's surly tones before he heads out to the SUV. I should go downstairs, but I hesitate, feeling awkward. I don't know how they all feel about me now. I open my door quietly and stand out on the upper balcony, looking down. They don't see me.

"I've never seen Dima so upset. Is Nikolai that bad?" Story asks from the living room. "I thought Ravil said he was going to be okay?"

Maxim grunts. "It's possible Dima's mood relates more

to a certain redhead who's under his skin." He peers into Nikolai's bedroom.

"Hey, guys." I lift an awkward hand and come down the stairs.

"Heyyyy, girl. How are you?" Story wraps me in a hug when I reach the bottom of the stairs, and I instantly feel better.

"Not great," I admit.

"We stopped in and fed your cat before we came. What's his name?"

"Mr. Whiskers. Thank you so much."

She looks me up and down. "I'm sorry, I should've thought to bring you some clothes. We brought food, though."

I tug on the stupid dress. I didn't put on the fishing shirt, since I don't have any shorts to wear it with. At least I can use it as a sleep shirt tonight, though. "Yeah. I'm about ready to cut a hole in a pillowcase to wear it instead."

Story smiles. "I'm sure you could rock a pillowcase, and I'm pretty handy with a pair of scissors if you want to try." She gestures to her black leggings, which have deliberate slashes up the thighs and down the sides of the calves, showing her pale skin. She's always a few measures of punk but underneath the counter-culture clothes, she's model-beautiful, which makes her mesmerizing. I think that is literally how Oleg fell in love with her. He got obsessed with watching her perform on stage.

Dima comes back in with another box that looks like it's filled with computer equipment, and he and Maxim shut themselves in the office.

Story heads toward the kitchen. "We did bring some groceries although Dima says he already picked some stuff up."

I follow her into the kitchen where Oleg had set the

cooler and help unload stuff. It's good—way more than the basics Dima bought. A couple of bags of salad mixes, fresh vegetables, and fruits, some deli meat for sandwiches, and an already roasted chicken.

"This is great, thanks."

She touches my arm. "Hey. Is there something going on with you and Dima? He seemed tense."

I turn it back around on her. I need information here. "Why does everything think there's something going on between us?"

Story shoots a glance to Oleg, who pulled up a chair at the table to sit. Oleg shrugs. "I don't know, it seemed like he was into you," Story says. "Am I wrong?"

Deciding what I really need here now is some girl talk, I tip my head toward the front door. "Want to go outside for a minute?"

"Sure." Story immediately follows me out, not hesitating or asking permission. She doesn't seem to know or think that I'm a prisoner here. But I doubt that she is a part of the bratva thing. She just happened to fall in love with one of its members—her giant, mute protector. The guy who looks at her like she's more beautiful than the moon itself.

We go outside onto the front porch and sit on the steps. "I'm seriously so mixed up. I could use a second opinion here," I admit.

"Okay, give me the scoop."

"I mean, I thought Dima was into me, too. He seemed interested. He booked a few massages, and he tips big. But that's when things just got weird."

"Weird, how?"

"He couldn't relax. He'd have a boner the entire time and just got progressively more grumpy with each session. I thought he must be attracted to me, but he never asked me out. And do you remember that time I came to your show?"

"Of course. You two came together, right?"

"No! That's just it. I asked him if he was going. I was trying to make it a casual date-thing, you know? But he said no. And then he turned up anyway and glared at everyone I talked to—it was so weird."

A slow smile spreads across Story's face. "He obviously is crushing on you."

I nibble my lip. I want to tell her the rest—everything. I'm dying for a sounding board here. "We sort of hooked up this morning. But then he said it was a mistake," I blurt.

Her smile fades. "Oh. That sucks." She pulls me into a hug I didn't know I needed.

I have to fight the tears back, or I will completely lose it.

"That's so weird. Is it...I mean, I don't know what happened to Nikolai, and I'm not supposed to know, but is it about that?"

"I don't know. Maybe. But it feels more like he has a girlfriend back in Russia or something. Have you heard anything about that?"

"I can ask Oleg. All I know is that the reason Dima booked a massage with you was because Nikolai said he was going to. Dima was really pissed at him—and he's usually so easy-going, I knew something was up."

"What?"

"Maybe they're fighting over you? Like they both like you, so Dima's going to let Nikolai have you? Or they both agreed not to pursue you? I don't know, I'm just spitballing."

I consider my conversation with Nikolai this morning. He didn't seem like he wanted me. But then again, he was sort of pumping me for information about what had happened between us. And Dima did seem pissed when he came in, and I was massaging Nikolai's hand.

Could Story be right? This is nuts!

The door opens, and Maxim and Oleg step out.

"Are we leaving already?" Story asks in surprise. Oleg nods. She gives me another quick hug. "Don't worry, I'll look after Mr. Whiskers. And if someone drives out here again, I'll pack you a bag of clothes."

"Thanks."

Story and I aren't that close, but it seems like we should be.

When I get back—provided I make it through all this —I'm going to seek out her companionship more often. Go to her shows. Maybe listen to her band practice—I know they have a studio in the building now.

I stand and walk inside, feeling much better. Nothing beats having a friend to talk to, even when nothing gets solved.

Maybe one thing got solved. I am certain Dima's into me.

So I don't have to cower like a scared little bunny.

I have power here, and I plan to use it.

Dima

As soon as I get my computer open and set up so it's untraceable, I video conference with Dr. Taylor to show him Nikolai's wound and give him an update, then I start hacking. Alex Volkov will be sorry he fucked with my family.

I check Natasha's phone and find he's called again, and sent an answer to my text.

I'm sorry, it says. *I didn't mean for things to go sideways like that. Please give me a call, so I can explain.*

Still nothing that completely clears Natasha.

I don't type an answer. I'll have to think of something I can say to bait him into revealing more, but first, I must do my homework, pulling on every thread I can find to unravel every secret Alex holds.

I start my cyberstalk. There's not that much. His unmarried mother gave birth to him in Champagne, Illinois six months after moving to the United States from Moscow. No father is listed on his birth certificate, but he's presumably Russian since she hadn't left the country before her trek to the U.S..

She has the equivalent of a Master's in Russian literature and taught Russian and Russian lit at the University of Illinois Champaign-Urbana and now at the University of Chicago.

I can't find any evidence that anyone pulled strings to get her a job, but she did have enough money to hire a lawyer to handle her immigration paperwork. I don't find evidence of financial hardship, nor do I find any hidden caches of riches.

Alex's cover story had been true, other than the false name he provided and the lie about his occupation. His undergrad was in criminal justice, and he was hired right out of college to work for the FBI. I'm surmising his fluency in Russian helped, especially with the rise in Russian *mafiya* cells across the country. They probably recruited him specifically to infiltrate one.

I get a sick feeling in my stomach when I admit the thought I'm trying to push away.

What if they hired him specifically to infiltrate *us*?

What do they want with Ravil? With us? Surely it's more than taking down our weekly poker game although

Nikolai does move huge amounts of cash as our bookie. He takes bets on all manner of things, online through dark web sites I have set up and in person.

I need to hack into the FBI, which isn't the easiest task. Things are kept behind layers and layers of firewalls. But I'll have to try. I set up some programs to start beating down the firewalls, then I move on to stalking my beautiful prisoner.

I sprout a chub just remembering what she looked like on her knees this morning, her berry lips wrapped around my cock. How she looked so damn willing. I was an asshole for letting her do that. The biggest *mudak* alive, but I'm finding it hard to be sorry.

Even if I can't have Natasha, I don't want to take that experience back. I'm glad I get to go to the grave knowing what it's like to have watched Natasha come. God knows I've fantasized about it long enough.

I research the hell out of her mom's trip to Russia, but everything seems totally above board. She's staying with her sister in St. Petersburg. I see no evidence that she's in hiding or has tried to disappear—not that anyone can disappear from me.

"Are you hungry?" The sound of Natasha's soft voice makes my cock lengthen down my leg. I try to find some of my earlier anger toward her to shield myself against her allure.

"No," I snap but make the mistake of turning to look at her. She freezes in the doorway where she's holding a plate with two sandwiches, a mixture of shock and hurt on her expressive face. "Yes," I change my mind when she starts to turn away. "*Spasibo.*" I thank her and hold my hand out for the plate, trying not to look her full in the face because I can't stand what her beauty does to me.

I want to pull her onto my lap, nuzzle her neck, and

soothe away all the harshness I've doled out to her, not just since Nikolai got shot but since she started giving me massages. Since she punctured the screen I use to keep a safe distance from anything emotional or sexual.

She looks at my screen over my shoulder, and I don't bother trying to hide it.

"You're stalking my mom." She sounds offended.

"I told you I had to check out your story, *amerikanka*."

She frowns at me. "And?"

I shrug. "I'm still investigating."

I take a bite of the sandwich she made, expecting her to walk out, but she doesn't. "Was one of these yours?" I ask with my mouth full, indicating the second sandwich.

She shrugs. "I can make another one. I didn't know how many you'd eat."

Gospodi, I'm such an asshole.

I hook my foot around the leg of the office chair Maxim had sat in and tug it closer. "Have a seat."

Damn. Did I really just invite her to sit with me? What am I thinking? I'm already way too obsessed with my memories of her punishment this morning.

She takes me up on it, scooting even closer to look at my screen as she picks up the second sandwich. She holds it in both hands but doesn't take a bite. "What would happen if you found out I did know about Alex?"

I whip my head around to stare at her. Her face is smooth, those sea-green eyes studying me. She seems wary but not terrified.

I narrow my eyes. "Why are you asking me that?"

She shrugs. "I want to know. Would Ravil… kill me?"

The idea sends a lightning bolt of fear straight up my spine, like the mere mention of someone killing her makes my body revolt. What *would* Ravil have us do to someone like Natasha? Would he order us to harm her?

No. In the few years my brother and I have been with his cell, I've never heard him give orders to hurt a woman, even if she's trouble.

"*Nyet.*"

"What would he do?" She stares down at the sandwich she still hasn't eaten.

I consider. Not so much because I think she deserves an answer but because I haven't thought it through yet, and I should in case it happens. "We'd have to flip you," I answer her honestly when I realize the only answer.

She takes a tiny bite of the sandwich and chews. "Flip me how?"

My gut churns as I consider the way we might flip her. We could threaten her mother. Throw them out of the building. Find anything dear to her and hold it hostage. There are a multitude of ways to use fear rather than violence. Ravil's practiced at the art of theatre when it comes to making things happen. We don't actually have to break that many laws—or that many fingers although that does still happen often enough.

But I couldn't stomach any of those things with Natasha. No, there's only one way I would allow her to be flipped, but it would require something of me that I've sworn I won't give.

I turn back to my screen and lie. "Pressure points."

She shivers. "Like what?"

"Enough questions, *amerikanka.*" I turn back to my screen, popping the last bite of the sandwich in my mouth.

"Why do you call me that?"

"Why do you think?" I say with my mouth full, playing the part of the asshole again. It's the only role that feels safe with her. I close out the search on her mother and start down the path I've been most looking forward to: antagonizing Alex.

"Are you judging me?"

I stop clicking keys and look her way. "What? No. Because you've become Americanized? Of course not. You grew up here. I admire how well you fit in, that's all. Nobody would even know you're Russian, except for your last name."

She sits back, finally digging into her sandwich. "I worked damn hard at it," she says. "It didn't just happen because I grew up here."

"Oh?" I give her a sidelong glance. I don't want to get sucked into her story—don't need any more fuel for my obsession with her, but I can't resist. "Why? Were you embarrassed to be Russian?"

"Pamela Harrison," she says like I should know who that is.

I swivel to face her. Now I need to know the whole story.

She licks a crumb of sandwich from her lips, and my dick twitches at the sight of her pink tongue. The memory of how she used it on me this morning is still fresh.

"She lived in my apartment building. We used to play together. It was the summer before fifth grade, and we spent nine hours a day together. And then school started. Someone made fun of my accent on the first day, and at lunch, Pamela pretended she didn't know me. Turns out, I was just her fall-back friend—good enough to play with at home, but at school, I was Russian garbage." As if the memory of it brought out Natasha's fifth-grade self, I hear the trace of her former accent for the first time. "You know what the worst of it was? I was so lonely that I still played with her at home. I let her use me. I was her fall-back friend for two more years until I finally had enough back-bone to cut her loose."

"Pamela Harrison was a cunt." I turn back to my

screen and pull her profile up on Facebook. "This one? She's an ugly cow—that's why she was jealous. Not because you had a beautiful accent."

Natasha lets out a small chuff of laughter.

It's the first time she's smiled or laughed since I dragged her here, and it does something squirmy to my insides. Dredges up guilt for taking away her smile, along with the desire to make her do it again.

"I will give her five parking tickets as punishment for her fifth-grade crime on our sweet Natasha," I pronounce as I open the Cook County police department records and use my back door access to get in.

"What?" The ring of laughter in her voice makes it all worth it. "You can do that? Oh my God!"

"Is that enough? Or should we punish her more severely?"

"You can't do that, Dima."

I steal a sidelong glance and catch her smile, which lights the whole office.

I start filing the false tickets. "I can, and I will. She deserves it. You know who else deserves a pile of unpaid parking tickets?"

Her smile falters. "Who?"

"Alex Volkov." I will make that asshole pay for nearly killing my brother.

"Oh." Natasha doesn't protest, she just sits and watches me work, chewing her sandwich slowly. "You're good at that."

"Damn straight." I manufacture a dozen unpaid parking tickets—enough to trigger a warrant to issue.

"You know what else is going to bite Alex in the ass?" I ask.

"What?"

"Not paying his taxes for the past three years."

Natasha gasps. "Dima, you can't—" She stops when I raise my brows and shoot her an *oh, really?* look. "I mean, what if you get caught? Won't they be able to trace this back to you? You're pretty much daring them to come after you now."

Is she worrying about me? About my safety? That's damn sweet of her.

I keep working. "I am taunting them, yes. But don't worry, I'm slippery as hell. They won't be able to track anything back to me."

I sense her gaze on my face rather than the screen, but I resist peeking to gauge her reaction to my handiwork.

"Where do you learn how to do this?" she asks softly.

"Vlad Popov, a bratva brother. I studied with him back in Russia. I heard he married into the Italian mafia and lives in Las Vegas now. Part of the Tacone crime family. But I have far surpassed his skills. At least in hacking. He was more interested in—" I stop myself. What the fuck is wrong with me? I can't go spilling bratva secrets to this girl. Especially not when she might be working with the Feds.

Except I'm almost certain she's not.

Still, I don't trust my gut when it comes to her.

"Sorry. I probably shouldn't ask about anything work-related."

"*Work-related*," I snort at the term. As if the bratva was a job, not an identity. A life. And for many, a prison. "Right." I finish changing Alex's tax returns and close out. "There. That will haunt him for a few years at least. Straightening out messes with the IRS is tricky business."

"I still don't understand," Natasha says. "Why did he shoot Nikolai?"

I resist the anger that surges—toward both Alex and her—and review the scene in my mind. I hate to admit what I think. "Honestly… I think when I came for you at the same time Nikolai came at him, he panicked. Maybe he thought I was a danger to you. Or he just couldn't process both events happening at once. It definitely seemed like panic rather than his training or premeditation."

"Yeah, he seems young. He's probably straight out of training, don't you think?"

I nod my agreement. "I don't like the fact that the Feds targeted you. You're in a precarious position now. You've admitted to the FBI that you know you live in a bratva-controlled building. They're going to continue to try to use you as leverage."

Finished with the sandwich, she sets her plate on the desk. "What's going to happen to me?"

I shrug. "Depends, *amerikanka.*"

"On what?"

"On what I find. On your behavior. On many things." My dick thickens again, thinking of her punishment this morning. It's so wrong, but I find myself hoping she'll misbehave. That I'll get to pin her wrists and smack her ass and listen to her sweet, choked cries.

"Is it up to you? Is that why Ravil said he'd let you sort of the rest of it out with me in private?"

I can't help myself. My lips curve into a tiny smirk. "That's right. I decide how and to what extent you are punished. So if you were wise, you'd keep a safe distance from me."

Her lips part in a pretty "O" but she doesn't look scared or upset. No, her pupils are dilated. She's turned on.

Blyad'. I need to rediscover my anger toward her because right now, I'm thinking of a hundred possible punishments, and they all involve her naked and at my mercy.

8

Natasha

Much of the heaviness lifts from my chest after talking to Story and getting Dima to at least converse with me. I saw glimpses of the real Dima today. The one who's not so on edge and pissed off at me.

Did he actually call me *sweet Natasha?* And give my childhood frenemy five parking tickets? I don't know anything about hacking, but it was obvious he has mad talent. It was impossible not to be turned on watching him change people's lives with a few strokes of his keys.

I shouldn't have let him do it, but there was no way I was going to refuse the small consideration he was giving me. Not when I've been so starved for any kindness from him.

There's chemistry between us, for sure. And he's resisting it. I just need to figure out why.

Or...I just need to get him to forget about his resistance.

I give him space for the rest of the afternoon, and he stays in the office and works. I stay attentive to Nikolai, getting him to swallow a little tomato soup, keeping his pain meds, electrolytes, and antibiotics going.

He blows me off when I make dinner—just some heated soup—telling me he'll eat later, so I eat with Niko-lai, then go upstairs and take a long bath.

When I get out, I'm pretty much ready to burn the cocktail dress. I wash my little G-string panties in the sink and hang them up on the shower rod to dry.

I pull on the ugly fishing shirt, which is a boy's size large. It doesn't even cover my ass. It's lame, even for a nightshirt. At least I won't have to sleep in the dress again tonight although I might be more comfortable naked.

That thought makes me all fluttery—like sleeping naked in the same cabin as Dima means something might happen. And after our brief truce this afternoon, I desper-ately want something to happen. He's been a dick, but now that the seed's been planted that it may not be about my big fuck-up—that he may be acting from a frustrated desire for me—the need to verify that hunch is huge.

I stand in front of the full-length mirror and take in my appearance. My hair is up in a messy bun. The shirt is tight across my breasts, showing the stiffened peaks of my nipples. It falls below my waist, about to the crease of my hips, so my bare and freshly shaved lady parts just peek out beneath.

Walking downstairs like this would be daring.

I'm not demure, but I'm definitely no sex kitten either. But unraveling the mystery of Dima's behavior makes it worth a try.

I head downstairs and walk past Dima where he sits with his laptop on his lap and some kind of action movie on the television. He doesn't look at me as I pass.

Dammit.

I head into the kitchen in search of something sweet to

eat--preferably chocolate. I search through the pantry, open and close every cabinet door, cataloging all the ingredients. And, if I'm honest, stalling. Because I don't want to head back upstairs without getting what I came down here for—and it wasn't just dessert. It's a reaction from Dima.

"What are you looking for?"

I pause without turning when I hear his voice behind me. He's in the kitchen with me. I make a show of opening an upper cabinet and standing on my tiptoes, reaching up to the highest shelves, which causes the already too-short shirt to ride up.

I hear Dima's sharp intake of breath. *"What are you doing?"* He sounds choked.

I still don't turn. This time I drop to my hands and knees to open a lower cabinet and stick my head inside. "I'm looking for chocolate." I continue with my hunt, sitting back and shifting to ransack the next cabinet, even though I've already searched them all.

"What—what are you wearing?"

I stand and slowly turn, arranging my expression into innocence. "The shirt you bought me." I slide my palms down over my breasts.

Dima's eyes flare. His fingers clench into fists at his sides.

"It's way too small." I had no idea playing the coquette could be so fun.

"*Gospodi*, Natasha. What—where are your panties?" He spits out the question like getting the answer is a national emergency.

"I washed them in the sink and hung them up to dry. I only have one pair, obviously." I bring my hands to my hips which lifts the shirt to my waist again.

Dima's gaze flicks between my legs, and he grows pale. When his gaze flies back to my face, something he sees there makes it harden. "Oh, I see." He strides toward me and catches my wrist, his brows down low. "I know what you're doing." He yanks my body roughly up against his. "You're being a cocktease."

I lift my chin and meet his blazing gaze with a defiant one of my own. *That's right. What are you going to do about it?* I close the half-inch distance that lies between our bodies, letting my nipples brush against his hard torso.

His blue eyes darken, a menacing heat radiating from his lethal body to mine. He cocks his head. "You may not like the consequences, *amerikanka*."

Try me. I slowly look down between our bodies to take in the bulge of his cock against my belly.

"Tormenting me will only get you punished again. Is that what you want? Should I put you on your knees to take care of this?"

With my gaze locked on his, I slowly lower to my knees.

"I don't like this side of you," he mutters as I reach for the button on his jeans.

Ignoring the sharp stab of pain his words produce, I resolve to keep the upper hand. Because I do have it. I watched his control crumble before my eyes. Noted the effect of my body on his. I lower his zipper, freeing his cock. Gripping the base, I part my lips, slackening my jaw to show my tongue but stop before I make contact. "You *do* like this side of me," I maintain, somehow making my gaze a challenge, even though I'm the one on my knees.

His cock surges in my fist, the purpled head already weeping with pre-cum. He wants to put it in my mouth. He wraps a fist around my messy bun, but when I resist him guiding my mouth forward, he yields. He's not the kind of guy to force a woman. I thought so, but it's still a relief to be sure.

"*Say* it," I demand. I flick the tip of my tongue over his slit, tasting the drop of his essence.

His breath rasps in through flared nostrils. His expression is stony, his eyes hard, but he mutters almost inaudibly, "You're right, *amerikanka*. There's no side of you I don't like."

Victory surges through me as powerful and pleasing as an orgasm. Maybe I do orgasm—I don't know. All I know is I engulf his cock with my mouth and take him as deep as I can.

He groans, his fingers tightening in my hair. This time when he tries to drive, I let him, aroused as hell by his desperation, his dominance. He pulls me forward and back over his cock and I suck on the outstrokes, my tongue swirling along the underside, caressing him.

"*Blyad',*" he curses in Russian.

I slide my hands up his muscular thighs, but when I move to cup his balls, he catches my wrist. "*Nyet,*" he says harshly. "Put them behind your back. This is punishment."

As if touching him with my hands would be a reward. But I love the order because when I hold my hands behind my back, I feel like his naughty little sex slave, and it hurtles me to the brink of my own orgasm.

I know I have a submissive personality, but I thought it came from immigrating to a new country as a child, from trying hard to fit in. Until now, I had no idea it was a sexual kink. I didn't know how wet I'd get being bossed around by the guy whose dick is in my mouth.

I suck his manhood like my life depends on it, pretending that it does because this idea of a sex act as punishment turns me *way* on.

He tightens his grip on my hair, holds my head still, and pumps in and out of my mouth. "Natasha," he rasps brokenly, giving himself away. Not that he didn't already.

There's no side of you I don't like.

Now that he's shown me his cards, he can't hurt me anymore. He can be a grumpy asshole all he wants, but I know the truth. He's into me. *Way* into me.

Now I just need to figure out why he's holding back.

"*Da...da...fuck.*" Dima shudders, his balls contracting. "Coming," he warns, releasing his hold on my head.

I don't stop sucking. In fact, I suck harder, glorying in the hot spurt of his cum in my throat, swallowing his essence down with pride.

"Jesus." He glares at me. "Get up." It's a harsh command, but it has no effect on me now.

He catches my elbow and hauls me to my feet. I don't know what I expect—he's not gentle, and he seems angry, but he puts both hands on my waist and lifts me to sit on the granite countertop of the L-shaped island.

My legs tremble, my breath heaves in and out of my chest. Dima picks up my knees, lifting and separating them until my feet stand on the cool counter, and I have to brace with my hands behind me.

His mouth is between my legs in milliseconds, and he's not slow or nuanced. It's more like an attack. His tongue lashes me open, drags through my juices. His lips find my clit, and he works it between them until he can suction his mouth over and suck.

I scream.

Not a ladylike cry. A full-on scream of shocked pleasure. I wriggle under the intensity of it, push at Dima's head, try to squeeze my legs closed.

Dima is unfazed. He's like a starved man, and I'm the main course. His fingers dig into my thighs as he holds my knees wide and goes to town on me. I orgasm within sixty seconds, but he doesn't let up. That's when he slides a thumb inside me and starts finger-fucking me, fast and hard. The heel of his index finger rubs over my clit with every plunge as he lifts his head and sweeps a gaze across the kitchen counter.

He leans over to grab something behind me. I turn, but then I'm lost, lying flat on my back, too stimulated to be able to hold my torso upright any longer. I prop myself on my elbows to see what Dima grabbed: a bottle of olive oil. He unscrews the cap with one hand, never stopping with the other hand, except to change to his index and middle finger, which he uses to stroke my inner front wall.

I shriek again when he finds my G-spot. "Dima!"

The pleasure is too much. It terrifies me, how out of control I feel. I wriggle and pant and then—

Oh, God.

Dima presses his other thumb—which he oiled up for me, against my anus.

I squeeze it up tight, my pelvis lifting off the granite countertop, and he spanks my pussy in punishment. "Nope. You're taking it in the ass for that little cocktease," he tells me at the same time he breaches my back hole.

"I didn't tease!" I cry out, my eyes rolling back in my head with the new sensation. It feels good—wrong—but so good. "I sucked you off."

"That's true." Dima's voice gentles, and so does his touch. He holds his thumb in my ass but doesn't move it. Instead, he lowers his head to slide his tongue slowly around my clit.

"Dima," I croon. I'm already desperate to come again. I'm trembling from the waist down. My legs somehow found their way onto Dima's shoulders, and I'm blind with need. No man has ever done *any* of these things to me. No anal play, no decent cunnilingus, definitely no kitchen countertop bringing me to orgasm in seconds kind of thing.

He penetrates my pussy with his other thumb, keeping his tongue on torture-duty with my clit.

My belly quivers as I suck in short, panting breaths. "Please," I beg. "Please, I need…"

Dima starts slowly alternating pumps—first in my ass, then my pussy.

I tremble from head to toe, each sobbing breath is a low keening cry.

"Oh, Dima."

He starts pressing both thumbs in simultaneously.

"No!" I exclaim in alarm although I mean *yes* because my orgasm is storming down the door, just about to pass-through—

He pumps faster.

"Yes!"

There's that moment of stillness—the zero point between inhale and exhale, between desire and pleasure, the pause just before the climax. The ceiling spins, my palms slap the cool countertop, and then the release hits. I cry out. My internal muscles squeeze and shake around both his thumbs.

"Dima, oh my God, Dima…"

I lie with my eyes closed, my breath sobbing in and out as I wait for the last aftershocks to pass.

Dima pulls both his thumbs out, and I hear him washing his hands in the sink. He dries them, and I sit up.

"Come here." He takes my waist and lifts me down.

"Um, we'd better sanitize the hell out of that counter," I say, suddenly embarrassed over what just happened.

Dima's lips twitch. "I'll do it," he mutters. His hands still rest lightly on my waist. He tugs the hem of my t-shirt down, even though it won't go lower. He reaches one hand behind me and squeezes my ass. His other hand comes to the front, and he lightly rubs his knuckle over my slit. "You keep this covered, or I'll put my cock between these milky white cheeks and fuck your ass until you're sorry."

A tremor runs through me—not of fear—of white-hot desire. I like Dima unleashed. I like seeing his passion show, to feel how hot it burns for me. I don't care if it comes in the form of punishment—hell, I think I actually love that part.

I catch his wrist when he starts to move it away and press his fingers over my dripping sex. That tremor told me I could orgasm again with almost no effort at all.

Dima doesn't leave me hanging. "You didn't get enough?" Two of his fingers dip into me, and my breath catches. I mold my hand over the top of his and grind against the heel of his hand to rub my clit. The ripple comes on within seconds, and my knees dissolve, leaving Dima to hold me up as my lips part on another choked cry.

Dima stares at me, seeming to forget to hide his fascination. *"Jesus."* He shakes his head, as if in awe. His voice sounds rough. "Do I need to put you back on that counter and eat that pussy until you scream?"

He phrases it as a threat, like that would be a horrible punishment, and it makes me squeeze around his fingers again, another little aftershock rippling through. He watches my face as if with avid interest. Without removing his fingers from inside me, he presses my ass back against the cabinets and reaches for something.

"Maybe you require something firmer." He spins me around to face the countertop, and I see he's grabbed a wooden spoon. My butt clenches in response.

"Do you?"

I realize he's checking for consent, at least I think that's what's happening. It's hard to sort it all out, but my head wobbles in my neck in a shaky yes. With his palm still

97

cupping my sex, fingers sunken inside, he smacks my ass lightly with the wooden spoon.

"Ooh." I squeeze around his fingers. My belly is all kinds of flutters. As I pant and wait for more, I'm seconds away from yet another orgasm.

"Did I make your punishment too enjoyable?" He spanks the same side a little harder. I clench my buttcheeks. It hurts, but I love it. I whimper and cover his hand with mine again.

"Uh uh. Hands on the counter." He gives me a sharp smack with the wooden spoon in the same place.

"Ow," I whimper, even though it didn't hurt that much. It's more that I want more. Need more. He's got me endlessly riding the edge of this orgasm.

He moves his fingers between my legs as he starts alternately popping each cheek with the spoon.

"Ow-*oh*…. Dima," I pant, wiggling under the steady onslaught. My butt's getting hot and tingly, the intensity matching the intensity of my desire.

"Hm." He pauses and plunges his fingers deeper inside me. "You feel how sopping wet that made you?"

"I… like it," I moan.

Understatement.

I need it. I crave it. I must have it all.

"How much do you like it?" He returns to spanking me, faster this time, maybe ten or more times. The moment he stops, I come.

He molds his body to my back and keeps working his fingers inside me until he's wrung out every last spasm and release.

"Whoa," I gasp when my breath has returned to normal.

Dima peels me away from the countertop and turns me

away from him, toward the stairs. "Go to bed, *amerikanka*." It's a gentle command, but definitely a dismissal.

Not wanting to ruin the deliciousness of my release with any speculation about what it means, I obey, walking away from him and not turning to look back until I reach the base of the stairs.

He's still standing there, watching me. His gaze is soft, sort of wondering, but when I catch it, he lifts his chin toward the stairs.

I draw a breath and turn back around. It takes all my concentration to make my shaky legs climb the stairs and get into bed.

I lie down and cup my heated ass, letting the endorphins flood through me, erasing all the tension from my brain and body. Ignoring the claw of loneliness that wants to rip into my heart.

9

Dima

It's pitch black out. I'm in the woods outside the cabin being chased by the Feds. I've hidden Nikolai in the Land Rover, and I'm leading them away from him, but I've lost Natasha. Do they have her? Is she with them?

Fuck, I don't know!

I run into a clearing and someone throws floodlights on. I skid to a halt, blinded. Out of the glare walks Alex, a gun in his hand pointed at me.

"Where's Natasha?" I demand.

"Natasha?" he gives a cruel laugh. "She's dead. Just like Alyona. You shouldn't have brought her here."

I THROW myself out of bed, trying to throw off the damn dream.

An hour later, I dump the plastic bags filled with every single piece of chocolate the convenience store had out on the kitchen counter. I left at dawn to drive out to the highway and get it, spurred by this inexplicable need to make sure Natasha's cravings are met.

Natasha's needs.

Holy. Mother. Of God.

Watching her come and come and come last night went beyond any of my wildest fantasies, all of which prominently feature her.

Who would've known? She doesn't come off as overtly sexual. She doesn't dress sexy. She dresses like an American teenager or college student. I guess I do, too, so maybe that means nothing. But her seeming lack of awareness of how goddamn beautiful she is has always been part of the appeal. It makes her seem young, innocent.

Makes me want to protect her with every gun I have— and I'm not usually the guy holding a weapon unless you count my computer. Which may be one of the most dangerous weapons Ravil wields, honestly.

And she still seems innocent to me, even after watching her string of sexy-as-fuck orgasms. She still seems untouched, even though I touched her.

Her soul is pure—maybe that's it.

She reminds me of Alyona, and I hate myself for mingling the two in my mind.

I shouldn't let Natasha overtake my memories of Alyona. Of how we lost our virginity together. Both of us fumbling in the back of the Lada in the crisp autumn air. Fogging up the windows until we had all the privacy we could desire. She let me take her clothes off. Laid across my back seat. I kissed her soft skin until she begged me to do more.

I wasn't rough or demanding like I was last night.

Gospodi, Natasha. Guilt crowds my chest. I was a

monster to her last night. I've been a monster ever since Nikolai got shot. No, if I'm honest, I was a dick even before that. From the moment she entered my bedroom with that massage table, I couldn't stop thinking of all the things I wanted to do with nothing but massage oil and bare skin between us.

I've pretended it's her fault—that she's the wicked temptation, luring me from the vows I made to Alyona on her deathbed, but in fact, the truth is the fault is only mine.

She's not wicked. She's sweet, even when she's purposely being a temptation. And she doesn't know about those vows.

Part of me wants to tell her—to explain why I can't. To admit my attraction, which has to be obvious at this point, and be honest with her. Tell her it can't ever happen. *We* can't ever happen.

But even that conversation feels like a betrayal to Alyona.

Like, the moment I bring her up to Natasha, I've forever sullied her memory. I've made her the other woman. The one I left behind for this new, shiny, *alive* one.

And I can't do that to Alyona.

She gave me everything. Her vulnerability. Her whole heart. I loved the person I was when I was with her because she loved me. I'm lucky—I've always had Nikolai. Twins are never lonely. But until Alyona, I was Nikolai's twin. He's the more social one. The funny one. He has charisma. I always let him do the talking for the two of us. Alyona made me feel like I was the special one. The one worth talking to. Spending time with. Planning a future with.

And then the cancer came.

She was so damn brave. I still remember how thin and

cold and bony her hand felt in mine when we sat together waiting for her chemo treatments. How she'd let me distract her and make her smile to pretend none of it was happening. The way she trembled when we finally talked about the end.

That was when I promised her I'd never love another. Never replace her. She was my first, and she'd be my last.

She had to face death at seventeen—*seventeen!* It's not too much for me to keep the promise I made to her.

I hear movement upstairs. Natasha is awake.

I washed my clothes last night, and now I leave my clean boxer shorts on the kitchen counter with the chocolate. I won't survive Natasha running around bare-assed, and so help me, if she lets Nikolai see her that way, I will have to kill him.

Or something.

I head into the office to return to the only thing that has ever made sense to me—cyber-stalking and hacking.

Behind a screen, I am still God. Even if I don't know my head from ass in this cabin.

I listen to Natasha. I hear her speaking softly to Nikolai, the sweet healer, checking in on her patient first. Then I hear sounds from the kitchen. The *pop* of the toaster oven. The opening and closing of the refrigerator.

I try not to picture the way she looked last night, standing on her tiptoes, that short shirt pulled up above her waist showing me the full moon of her pale ass.

That pale ass I turned red.

Fuck. Did I force her? There was something harsh and punitive to what went down, but it was consensual…. Wasn't it? I was sure last night, but after barely sleeping because I couldn't stop replaying what happened, it all feels fuzzy now.

She's overly agreeable. The type you could easily take advantage of.

I mean, I know I got her off. She was sopping wet. She came around my fingers over and over again.

But is she sorry today? Does she feel used? Taken advantage of? Forced?

For once, the screen holds no answers for me. I can't cyberstalk her to get an answer to this question. To make sure she's okay.

Dammit.

I push back from my chair and get up.

I find her sitting at the long farm table. She's still in the fishing t-shirt—braless, of course, because heaven holds no mercy on me. I can't tell whether she's wearing my boxers or not, but a quick glance at the counter shows me they're gone.

"Thanks for the chocolates." Her gaze is warm and soft on me.

I shrug, not taking a seat. "I didn't know what kind you like, so I bought them all."

Her lips twitch in amusement. "That was good thinking. I would've hit anything last night, but I'll start with the Heath bar. I'll eat them all, for sure. The Hershey bar will probably be low on my list. I'm actually a chocolate snob. I go for the gourmet eighty-five percent dark chocolate kind of bars."

"Gourmet bars first, then Heath. Got it." Dammit, what am I doing? I'm not her boyfriend. I won't be buying her more chocolates. "I didn't know you had a thing for chocolate."

"You don't know a lot of things about me."

Not true.

At least, I probably know far more than she thinks. But I hadn't gone so far as to stalk her grocery choices.

"It's my stress go-to, and, um, this is stressful." She lifts her hands with a wry scrunch of her nose. It's adorable.

For some reason, my heart beats like it's pumping blood for two people right now. "Natasha, I just, ah…"

She lays her slice of buttered toast down on her plate and looks up at me expectantly.

"Are you okay? After last night? I mean…" *Blyad'*. I plow a hand through my hair. "Did you feel forced?"

"Well, I think that was kind of the game we were playing, right?"

Bozhe moi, this girl. So calm and cool about it. So freaking mature.

Relief washes over me. Then my brain goes into overdrive. Is that a game she knows? One she's played before? Fuck, I don't even want to know the answer because I want to kill any guy who got rough with her in the past. And I was rough. I probably left marks on her ass spanking her with that spoon.

"Yeah. I just wanted to make sure you were okay."

Her gaze drops, and she starts scraping at the polish on her fingernail—her nervous tell.

My stomach bottoms out like I'm on the dip of a roller-coaster. I will karate chop my own throat if I traumatized this girl.

"I'm good. I mean, I liked it." My relief is short-lived because she goes on, "I'm less okay with you calling it a mistake every time. That makes me kind of queasy."

Queasy. Dammit. That sounds like shame. Or humiliation. Nothing she deserves. I have to fix this fuck-up.

I stride over to her and pull the chair beside her out. She makes eye contact when I sink into it. "Natasha…"

I don't know what to say. How do I explain without betraying Alyona?

"I, uh, I liked it, too. I like you… a lot. But I can't be in a relationship. So I don't want to lead you on that way. That's the only reason I said it was a mistake."

She nods slowly, studying me like she's examining my story for cracks.

"I may think it was a mistake, but I'm also not sorry," I admit.

She works to swallow and turns her face back to her plate, picking up her toast.

I take the hint and get up. As I walk toward the office, I hear her say softly, "I'm not sorry, either."

Her words fall over my head and shoulders like one of those nets that drops from the trees. It's light, seemingly harmless, but when it closes around me, it traps me into new thoughts.

Thoughts of more.

Wondering if it could happen again without the giant ship of my entire identity sinking to the bottom of the ocean.

Natasha

He bought me chocolates.

Not just a few pieces. The guy literally must've bought out the whole store.

Maybe it was out of guilt—it sounds like he was worried I'd felt forced. As if I hadn't been the one to drop to my knees and unbutton his jeans.

He revealed so much about himself this morning. Not just the conversation saying he couldn't have a relationship. I already surmised that much. And yes, I'm kicking myself for not asking why. I didn't want to show any disappointment or hurt, so I just swallowed the statement and let it sit in the pit of my stomach, making it impossible to finish my breakfast.

But the purchase of the chocolates, the checking in with me—those actions prove that he is the guy I thought he was. He may be acting like a grumpy bastard right now, but he's safe. He's kind.

And I still want him.

Am I an idiot for setting my targets on a guy who tells me he's unavailable?

Most certainly.

But he's also admitted he likes me a lot.

And I like him a lot.

And none of that is even about the off-the-charts sex we've had. Last night was life-changing for me. I found out things about myself I never knew, and I will never be able to approach sex the same way again. To think, we haven't even gone all the way yet! If we're this good in an office and a kitchen, I can't imagine how explosive we could be in a bedroom.

But the best thing is that I don't even need that.

Dima feels right to me.

When I'm with him, I feel like I can be myself. I suppose that's why I could give myself over sexually—I didn't hold back or edit myself. I let go, and the entire world exploded.

Dima feels like mine. Like we belong together. There's an ease between us—like we're an energetic match. That's what I'd felt with him from the first day we met. I'd made a note to myself that if I ever was in trouble, he was the bratva member I'd go to for help. He was the one I knew I could trust.

Then things got weird, but now, I know what that was about.

He recognizes what we have, too. And for some reason that I need to discover, he thinks we can't be together.

Well, I'm not going to stop pushing. Or tempting. And if he wants to punish me—well, we both know how that will end.

With a whole lot of sexual satisfaction on both our parts.

I'm not giving up. I'm seeing this thing through.

Dima is worth fighting for.

Dima

I wake in the night to the sound of something outside the cabin. I leap out of bed and palm the Glock on the bedroom dresser. I'm in the master bedroom where Nikolai's recovering. Even though he seems like he's doing okay, I'm not willing to sleep in a separate bedroom. Like he might stop breathing just because it's night or something.

I hear another sound—right outside the French doors that open to the deck.

I silently turn the lock on them, twist the handle, and nudge the door open, all the while I'm on an internal rampage against myself for not having figured out Alex's every secret. Because it seems there must be something more to him than a trigger-happy Federal agent.

Something feels off. Very off.

The door opens silently—it's solid and well-built. All the glass in this place is bullet-proof, so me opening the door might not be my brightest move. But fuck, my brother is lying half-dead in the bedroom, and I have an innocent female upstairs to protect.

A light splash of water draws my attention to the sunken hot tub a few paces from the French doors.

Blyad.'

The innocent female I thought was sleeping upstairs is in my hot tub.

Naked.

Moonlight glints off her pale skin.

"You nearly got your head shot off, *amerikanka*," I say softly, putting the safety back on the Glock.

I should go back inside and leave her to her soak, but I can't seem to make my body turn around. Instead, I walk past her, careful not to look, and stand at the deck, facing out. I place the Glock on the railing.

"You wouldn't shoot me." Her answer is just as soft. She didn't seem startled—like she expected me to come.

Is she playing games again? Moonbathing nude where I'm sure to find her?

Probably.

Fuck.

I definitely need to turn around and go back inside.

Get the upper hand and show her I won't be manipulated.

But I don't move. I promise myself not to look at her. I saw nothing but her bare shoulders from the back. I won't let myself turn and drink in the perfection of her youthful breasts. Because I'm sure they are as perfect as that pretty pink pussy I had my tongue on last night.

"Did you know there was a hot tub out here?" Her voice sounds a little rusty.

"Yeah." I won't look at her. I *will not* turn around.

"It's so perfect—to soak in total luxury surrounded by nature. The smell of pine and earth. The moonlight. I'll bet it's a dream in the winter, too."

I never considered the hot tub anything other than

another amenity Ravil put in because he has money to burn. We have one on the roof of the Kremlin, too. I've been in it a few times, but I don't make it a practice. I don't really pay attention to shit like that.

I have to swallow back the offer on the tip of my tongue to bring her back here in winter.

I won't be seeing her in winter. I'm not seeing her now. I need to make that clearer.

"Why did Ravil send us here?" she asks.

"In case there was heat," I explain, even though sharing bratva secrets is totally forbidden. I don't know what the fuck is wrong with me. "Even though we didn't do anything wrong. Alex should be the one hiding out somewhere. He would be if he were smart."

A little splash comes from the hot tub, and I'm suddenly dying to know what she's doing in there.

"Is-is he in danger? I mean—"

Anger that she's worried for his welfare makes me gnash my teeth. "No more questions, Natasha. I've already told you far more than I should have."

"You've told me nothing." A note of defensiveness rings in her voice.

"I should have put a bag over your head driving here."

I hear her suck in her breath at that and after a long pause, she says, "I'm glad you didn't."

Trying to shut her down more, I snap, "We're here to isolate you until we know what the fuck is going on."

"And do we?"

I laugh humorlessly at her choice of *we* instead of *you.* "Not yet, *amerikanka.* But I intend to unearth every last secret you or Alex have ever held."

She's quiet for a moment, then she says, "I don't know why, but that kind of turns me on."

My snort of laughter surprises me. "You like being the object of my investigation?"

"Yes."

Damn, this girl. If she only knew how long I've been cyberstalking her.

The deck seems to tilt as the dark trees murmur and shake around us. A sharp sense of ownership snaps into place between us. An exchange of power she willingly handed over.

She's baring herself to me. Offering herself up. Her life to my examination. Her body to my touch. Her innocence to my dark vengeance.

I draw a deep breath trying to draw back from her siren's song. I shouldn't want to master her. To be the man she surrenders to.

And yet the memory of Alex walking in that room with her makes me want to punch his teeth out. I don't deserve this honor, and even if I did, I couldn't take it. But no fucking way I think another man is worthy of her, either.

"There are a few facts I haven't been able to ferret out about you, Natasha."

"Like what?" Her voice is light. Teasing. She's playing a game.

She's obviously decided she's safe with me. I should be comforted by that fact. It proves her innocence in all this. Yet the bastard in me thinks I should keep her scared. Keep her on edge, so her fear provides the barrier between us that I can't seem to keep up.

"Why did you quit your job as an EMT?"

"Your computer couldn't tell you that?"

"It delivers facts not reasons."

"What's your guess?" Her voice is musical. Gentle. Like we're lovers having a midnight soak together and not a prisoner and her prison guard.

"My guess… is that you saw some things you couldn't stomach."

She draws in an audible breath before she answers, "Exactly." The force of her answer makes me turn around before I can catch myself.

Because I need to see her face. I'm sorry when I find what I expected to see—a bleak, haunted expression.

"Did someone die?"

"Yeah."

"Old or young?"

"There was more than one. It was five in a row." Her voice breaks a little.

I step closer, despite my resolve, and crouch at the edge of the hot tub. I'm in my jeans because I gave her my boxer shorts, but I took my shirt and socks off.

"Can you believe that?" She gives a watery laugh. "Five in a row that we couldn't save in time. Young, old. There was a heart attack victim, a gunshot wound, a toddler who'd choked on a hot dog and died before we got there. We lost them all. And that's when I knew I'd chosen the wrong area of focus."

I catch her choice of words, and I'm intrigued. "And massage is the right area?"

She gives an embarrassed little chuff. "Well, it's closer." She sounds defensive, and that bothers me.

I sit cross-legged on the deck. I'm on the opposite side of the hot tub from her—safe enough distance—and my interest isn't dick-led for once. I've been chewing on this mystery of her career change for a while now.

"Hold on." I put my palm up. "Why did you take that as an insult? Who made you think massage therapy wasn't a worthy substitute?" As far as I can tell, she's an amazing therapist. She finds all my tight spots without being told. If it weren't for the iron erections they produced, I'd feel great after her massages.

Her bowtie lips part in surprise. "I… I don't know. Maybe my mom, but she never actually said that." She lifts her slender shoulders which has the unfortunate effect of showing me the tops of her breasts as they come out of the water. "Maybe me." The words fall heavy, like stones dropping into the water between us, and her lips twist like she's tasting something bitter. Her gaze is suddenly far away.

"What would you rather do or be?"

She looks at me for a moment, and I'm sure there's an answer. She knows exactly what she wants to do.

"Tell me," I prompt, hating that she's holding it back from me.

"I wanted to be a naturopath."

I make a mental note to research that. I've heard the word but have no idea what it actually means.

"Why *wanted* past tense? What's stopping you?"

She lets out a little puff of air. "Money. I applied to schools after I got my undergrad, and I got in, but I didn't get any scholarship offers. The thing is, I still have a pile of debt from my student loans from undergrad, and there aren't any schools in Chicago, so it's not just tuition I'd need to pay for, but room and board, as well. It's just not feasible."

I frown. "You must know Ravil gives microloans to members of our community all the time."

"I can't take on any more debt," she snaps, but I hear the tears of frustration behind the anger, so I hold up my hands in surrender. "Right. I understand."

"I'm sorry." She sinks lower in the water, dipping until it touches the bottom of her chin. Like she wants to disappear.

I don't want her hiding, so I expose my own flaws. "I actually have no idea what a naturopath is."

Her easy smile relaxes her whole face and sets my world on fire. "It's like a doctor, but using holistic and alternative medicine to treat illness. It would be a four-year program, followed by a two-year residency."

"Ah. That makes sense."

She tilts her head, her red-blonde locks trailing in the water. "What does?"

"The appeal of natural medicine. Considering who your mother is."

She nods. "Right. I grew up attending home births with my mother. We only use folk remedies when we are sick, even though my mother can write prescriptions now. I've seen time and again how the body balances itself when given the right support."

"I remember the poultice you made for Oleg when his leg was infected. He healed quickly. That's probably a dying art."

Seeing her face shine at my words does crazy things to my stomach.

"I believe in the body's natural ability to heal, and I'm fascinated by all the alternative methods that are out there. I mean, I've seen women who couldn't conceive get pregnant using Chinese herbs and acupuncture. Did you know Chinese medicine doesn't believe in infertility except in a tiny percent of cases?"

I shake my head, entranced, not so much by her words, but by her enthusiasm. The light that shines behind her face is brighter than the moon.

"Are you interested in Chinese medicine?"

"Well, I love it, but I don't think acupuncture is my thing. I just want to learn everything, to be honest. And I believe Western medicine has its place, but there are so many remedies that have fallen by the wayside because they don't have a patent and big pharma behind them, you know?"

"I'm sure." My mind is already working overtime trying to figure out how I can help her make all this happen, legally or illegally. Natasha has a passion, and she shouldn't have to give up on her dreams because they are impractical. Or because she doesn't have the support she requires.

Besides, getting her out of Chicago—sending her safely away to naturopathy school for four years—suddenly seems like the best possible solution for my sanity. A compromise for the burning need I have to take care of her—to infiltrate her life and turn us both inside out in the process—without breaking my vow to Alyona.

"You can get in the hot tub, you know." Her voice is suddenly soft. I can't decide if it's shy or teasing.

"No chance." I climb to my feet.

She splashes a little water across my feet. "Why no chance?"

"You're in there." I speak as I walk to the French doors, my back to her. "Naked. Wet. Slippery." My jeans are way too tight by the time my hand rests on the door handle, like my verbal acknowledgment of her hot little siren body makes her even harder to resist. "And I have about nine hundred eighty ideas of what I could do to it." I yank the door open and step through, pulling the door shut without looking back.

"Dima?" she calls to me just before it clicks shut.

I stop, dragging in a tortured breath. Fuck. I turn. "*Da?*"

"I forgot a towel. Could you bring me one?"

A growl of disapproval sounds in my throat. She's manipulating me again. I try to cloak myself in annoyance while the thrill of anticipation wings around me, whipping me into a frenzy. I point a stern finger at her. "Only if you stay in that tub."

She gives a quick nod, her face pure innocence, and I should have known better.

Or maybe I do.

Maybe I knew what she would do from the moment she asked for the towel, and I wanted that outcome. My punishment. Both our rewards.

This filter of the prisoner and her keeper that allows me to justify things I have no business doing.

Because, of course, when I bring the towel to her, she stands up out of the hot tub, water streaming from her slick body, steaming around her in a cloud.

Her breasts are perfection—pale, peach-tipped beauties with freckles that dip from her breastbone down between them.

I snap the towel around behind her and use it to yank her up against my body roughly. "What did I tell you about staying in the hot tub?" I make my voice a menacing snarl —so unlike any voice I ever use with anyone in my life. Especially a beautiful woman.

Maybe this helps me believe it isn't real. What I am about to do to her. What I already did twice before. I'm playing a role, enacting a part for the bratva. I'm not falling for a woman.

I'm not giving myself to her.

I can't offer that.

Her wet hands brace against my bare chest, her soft lips part.

I walk her backward, loving the mingle of fear and excitement in her gasp, her widened eyes. Her calves hit the back of a lounge chair, and I use the ends of the towel to keep her from falling back. "Turn around." My words are smoky. Dangerous.

She spins obediently, and I push her to her knees on the cushion. She grips the back of the chair. Her ass has a few marks from last night, and that gives me pause.

Hurting Natasha was never my plan.

"Spread your knees." My guttural bark oddly fits out here in the darkened forest.

Again, her enthusiasm couldn't be doubted. Natasha, for all her sweetness, loves the kink. Somehow it makes me even crazier for her.

I gather her wet hair in a bundle and tug her head back. "You like to be punished." I slap lightly between her legs.

She gasps and shivers, letting out a little note that sounds like, "ooh."

I spank her pussy again. The wet flesh slides under my fingers, inviting them to linger. A few more slaps, and then I accept the invitation, pushing my middle finger through her folds, seeking her clit. I find it and circle once, twice. I press my thumb over her asshole as I screw one finger into her. She's wet—sopping wet.

I pull my fingers out and give her ass a light spank. "You're lucky there's no olive oil out here, *amerikanka,* or I'd put my cock right here." I press on her anus, making it flutter against the pad of my thumb. "I guess I'll have to make you pay another way."

It's wrong—ever so wrong—but I unzip my jeans. My cock is hard as steel for her, throbbing to be used for the benefit of us both.

"I don't have condoms, but I'm clean," I tell her as I drag the head of my cock through her juices. I'm looking for consent.

Maybe I'm hoping she'll spook.

She doesn't. "I'm on birth control."

I ignore the part of my brain that wants to analyze who she went on it for.

She wants me to fuck her.

I grip her hair again, making her back arch when I pull. "You need me to show you what happens when you test me?"

"Yes," she breathes.

Foolish girl. Foolish, beautiful, darling girl.

I can't help myself. I shove into her and my mind short-circuits at how good she feels. Her delicious wet heat. The way her tight channel hugs my member like a glove. It's been so long since I've had sex, I'd forgotten how incredible it feels. But this doesn't compare to those early fumbles of my youth. Everything is different. I'm a different man. Hardened by violence. Removed from life. I'm not a gentle lover. I'm not attentive, except to make sure she's still enjoying it. That she still consents. I'm an animal, staking a momentary claim.

And because it's so different, it seems allowed.

I slam in, fucking her hard.

She arches that slender cat-back of hers, pushing her ass to meet my thrusts, taking me deep. My balls slap against her soft flesh. Every smack satisfies me in a way I don't understand. I'm not a sadist. At least I didn't think so. But the heady sense of power she offers with her surrender makes me high.

Shame at the mental contortions I made to allow myself to do this mingles with the high, and I get even more brutal with my pounding, changing my grip to hold her hips and taking shorter strokes.

Natasha starts to vocalize her need—short gasping cries that make me even more desperate to fuck the hell out of her. "Dima!"

I both love and hate when she says my name.

It makes it personal but sounds so damn perfect at the same time. Hell, this is personal. Me pretending it's not is jacked.

It's cruel to Natasha.

Unfair to Alyona.

Torture to me.

"Come, *amerikanka*," I order. I have no idea why I think I can command a woman's orgasm, but she squeezes around my dick like she's trying to obey.

"*Blyad.*'" Heat spikes at the base of my spine. I pump faster.

"*Dima.*" She sounds alarmed now.

I know the feeling. The pressure before the release. My movements get jerky as I slam in and out, hurtling to the edge of the precipice. And then I'm catapulted over it. I slam in hard and come.

Natasha reaches between her legs to rub her own clit and tangle my fingers with hers, nudging her out of the way. As soon as I take over she comes. I bump in and out a few times to help bring it to a full finish.

I pull out and give her ass a resounding slap—hard enough to make her flinch. "Bring your own towel next time," I tell her, my voice deep and rough. I put my dick away, and then I go into my room and shut the door in true asshole fashion.

Natasha

I wake to the sound of rain. The clock beside the bed says I slept until 9:30 a.m., which is far later than it seems because the sky outside is grey with a summer storm. It's incredibly cozy. I want to pretend we're here at this beautiful, luxurious cabin on a weekend getaway. That we have to stay in and play games together today, but when the rain lifts, we'll go for a walk in the forest and enjoy the scent of rain on pine.

I head downstairs. Dima's in the office. I pass by to check on Nikolai, who I find awake.

Yesterday we video chatted with Dr. Taylor to show him Nikolai's wound, and he said everything was progressing well.

"Are you wearing Dima's boxer shorts?" he asks.

"Yeah." I tug on the hem. It's one thing tempting Dima, it's quite another to be inappropriate in front of his twin. "Oleg and Story brought out groceries and computer stuff, but they forgot to send us with clothes."

"At least yours weren't cut off you." Nikolai flicks his

gaze down to his shirt, which was cut to the armpits for surgery. "So does that mean Dima's free-balling it?" he smirks.

I ignore the question, but he starts singing the lyrics to Tom Petty's "Free Falling," replacing *falling* with *balling.*

I try not to smile, even though he is hilarious. "I guess you're feeling better?"

"Just loopy from these drugs. So, should I just pretend I didn't hear you screaming outside my room last night?" Nikolai says casually as I take his temperature. A strangled sound comes from my throat, and his lips twist into a grin. "Next time, you two could move a little farther away from the door, no?"

"Sorry. It wasn't exactly planned."

"No?" Nikolai lets disbelief ring in his voice.

My face grows warm.

"I'm not judging. I'm the opposite of judging, Natasha. I've been trying to get Dima to hook up with you since day one."

"Hook up?" I echo, not sure I like the sound of that.

"Sorry. Did that offend you?" Nikolai winces as he tries to sit up more.

I help him lean forward and adjust the pillows behind his shoulders. I hate how frail he seems.

"May I ask you a question?" Without waiting for an answer, I ask it. "Why can't Dima have a relationship?"

Nikolai shakes his head slowly. He's still pale, and his face needs a shave. "Is that what he said?"

"Stop turning my questions into questions."

"What exactly did he say?"

"He said, *I can't be in a relationship. I don't want to lead you on.*"

"*Blyad.*'" Nikolai grunts and scrubs a hand across his

face. "Then I suspect… he made a promise to a dead girl. And my brother doesn't break his promises."

I stare at him in horror. *A dead girl.* The ring he wears on his finger. Why had it never occurred to me that he wears it as a remembrance?

"Who was she?"

Nikolai shakes his head. "It was so long ago."

I don't know why I want to burst into tears—whether it's for me or for him. I resist the urge.

"Natasha…" Nikolai's blue gaze—so identical to Dima's—rests on my face, and he sees what I'm trying to hide. He reaches out and takes my hand. "At some point, the pain of resisting you will become greater than the pain of betraying his ghost. I hope… I just hope you can forgive him for the mess he's making in the meantime."

I blink rapidly, the patchwork of bandages covering my heart loosening and peeling back. It's not Dima asking for forgiveness but Nikolai on his behalf. It's his twin admitting that Dima's treated me unfairly.

It soothes the pain, but it doesn't give me hope.

Now I understand, at least, what Dima's hangup is. But I don't want to make him break a promise to a dead girl. I no longer want to play temptress.

Not with what's at stake for him. His loyalty. His love.

It's not fair to either of us to continue with this craziness.

I remove my fingers from Nikolai's grasp and turn away. "Of course, I forgive him," I say as my heart liquifies and leaks out of my chest.

I forgive everything.

And I need to move on.

∼

Dima

I spend the morning solving Natasha's student loan problem. My first instinct is to simply erase the digital existence of any such loan. But even though I'm one hundred percent sure of myself and my ability to never get caught, I know Natasha would not like the idea of having stolen her education.

So I transfer money from my savings to pay off her student loans—about forty thousand in all.

Next, I hack her email to find every place she applied to school to study naturopathy and then cross-check all the schools with a list of the best. Even though it's summer and the application deadlines for this fall were nine months ago, I put together her application materials and start the process of hacking into the application files of the best schools around. I'm not sure how exactly to make it happen, but I hope I might submit the applications in a way that makes them seem like they've been there all along, then maybe send a few with choice emails from important Deans at the school or something to check on their status.

I have to make this perfect. She needs to not only get into all these schools but to get scholarships, too, because I doubt she'll take another loan out. It's not an impossible task. Her grades are good. Mostly A's, a few B's. I go into her undergraduate transcript and change the B's to A's. Her MCAT score is good.

I find the essay she wrote last time. It was decent. A little plain. I send it off to Lucy, Ravil's wife. Lucy is a brilliant attorney with top-notch writing skills. She might be able to retool the essay into something spectacular. That's my hope, anyway. I send her my ideas for it—that it opens with a story about attending births with her mother and the miracles she saw and tie together that natural act with the body's natural healing, or something like that. I don't know—I can't write in English past a sixth-grade level, but I'm sure Lucy can make it brilliant.

When I finish, I cancel every debit and credit card Alex has just to fuck with him.

He's tried calling Natasha about a dozen times, and every time he does, I come back to my workstation to mess with him some more. His latest text says, *I really did enjoy our time together--I wasn't faking that.*

As much as that makes me want to kill him in a hundred messy ways, it's definitive proof that Natasha had no idea he was playing her. Something I can show Ravil if he questions her loyalty.

NATASHA CORNERS me in the office in the afternoon. The rain that's been pouring down all morning just abated to a sprinkle. "May I have my phone back?"

She's in the same ridiculous fishing shirt and my boxer shorts, somehow managing to make the outfit look both chaste and pornographic at the same time.

"No."

She lets out a surprised puff of air. "Why not?"

"I haven't sorted things out yet with your boyfriend." I'm being a dick. A total baby.

She said she hasn't had sex with him. She told me she wore the dress for me, not him, and she'd brought him to force my hand. I shouldn't still feel threatened by this guy.

Maybe it's the fact that I can't claim Natasha as my own that makes me crazy possessive of her. Knowing she's fair game—or will be the moment we leave this cabin and she returns to her life—makes me want to commit murder.

Her jaw firms. "He's not my boyfriend." She puts her

hands on her hips in a stance that unfortunately makes my dick hard. She's so damn cute when she's mad. "I *need* my phone, Dima. I have to cancel the massage appointments I had scheduled this week. And what if my mom called?"

Guilt gives me a twinge of pain under my sternum. I rub it. "She called yesterday. But I texted her to say you'd give her a call today."

"What?" She throws her arms out in exasperation. "So when were you planning on giving me my phone to make that promised call?"

I scowl at her. "Well, I promised that before loverboy started lighting up your phone."

She rolls her eyes and holds her hand out expectantly. "Give me the damn thing."

I can't decide if I love or hate that she's figured out I'm no danger to her at all.

"Fine," I grit. "But you make your calls in my presence, and then you hand it back."

She shakes her head and sighs. "Whatever."

I place the phone in her hand. "Stay in this room," I warn her.

She turns her back to me but doesn't leave. She leaves messages with three clients saying she had a family emergency and had to leave town, then calls her mother.

"Hi Mom," she says when the phone connects.

I hear a stream of Russian from the other end, and then Natasha answers in English, "No, everything is fine… my date?" She turns and looks at me.

My nostrils flare.

"Not great. I'm not seeing him again." She holds my gaze as she says it, like she's trying to prove something to me.

As satisfying as that may be, I have no right to demand

anything with her dating life. I'm not her boyfriend. I can't be. I gave my heart to another.

I can't distinguish Svetlana's words, but her tone sounds coaxing like she wants Natasha to give it another try.

I turn away, so Natasha won't see my glare, my fingers curling into a fist.

"He was using me, Mama. He wanted—" she breaks off when I whirl and give her a warning look. "We just weren't a good match, that's all."

There's a little more back and forth, Natasha asks after her aunt, her mom wants to know if she watered the plants, and then she hangs up.

She hands the phone back to me with a withering look. "Did I pass the test?"

An apology is on the tip of my tongue—I definitely owe her one, but just then her phone lights up with another call from Alex, and I grind my teeth, wanting to smash the damn thing.

My phone rings at the same time, and when I see it's Ravil, I answer, watching Natasha sashay out of the room with her head held high.

"What have you found out about Alex Volkov?"

"Nothing I haven't already told you."

"What about his taste in women? Has he dated much? What kind of women does he like?"

"He had a couple of girlfriends in college. Look like nice, normal girls. One played soccer, one became a teacher. Why?"

"Do you think he has real feelings for Natasha? What has she told you about him?"

Well, fuck. I haven't exactly gotten her to open up about their past dates since I was busy stomping my feet like a toddler at the fact that they even happened.

"Why?"

"He just showed up at the Kremlin—alone. Maykl stopped him from getting past the foyer, of course, but he was throwing a fit about needing to see Natasha. Said he'd come back with a warrant to search her place if we didn't let him up there to see her." Ravil pauses, and his voice softens. "Lucy went down and handed him his balls on a platter."

I relax a little. "Good."

"She told him we have footage of what he did, and she'd be happy to send it to every news station in the city, along with every supervisor at the FBI, and then she told him to lawyer up because we'd be filing a civil court case against him."

"Did he leave?"

"He left. But you need to have Natasha call him. Maxim and I suspect he's the hero-type, and he fears for her safety. I want her to call him off before he gets that warrant."

Of all the fucking orders from my *pakhan*.

Dammit.

"I'll have her do it now," I promise, even though speaking the words feels like choking glass.

"Text me when it's done."

"*Da, pakhan.*"

I stalk out of the office in search of her. I suppress the urge to bellow her name in rage and make her come running. This isn't her fault.

Actually, yes it is.

I find her in the great room, standing at the giant window like she's watching the raindrops trickle down the glass.

"*Natasha.*" Damn. I need to dial it back. It already sounds like I've come for her head.

She whirls, her beautiful eyes wide.

I hold her phone out. "You have to call Alex."

She makes a *pfft* sound. "I'm not calling Alex."

"No. You are. Ravil's orders. He showed up at the Kremlin to see you and threatened to get a search warrant for your place."

She doesn't reach for the phone, just eyes it suspiciously. "So what am I supposed to say?"

"Just let him hear your voice and know you're alive."

"Fine." She snatches the phone from my palm and opens her contacts. When she enters *Alex*, it doesn't come up.

"Oh yeah. I changed his name to *douchebag* in your contacts."

She gives me a withering look.

I shrug. "You can change it back to *loverboy* when you regain your phone privileges."

She glares at me. "My phone privileges? Seriously? When are you going to get over it?"

"When my brother no longer has an IV in his arm and can get out of bed," I shoot back, which is a low blow because one thing I am certain of is her despair over what happened to Nikolai.

She gives me her back, which does nothing to hide her face since I can see her reflection in the windows.

"Alex?" She sounds a little breathless when he answers, and my molars grind.

"Natasha! Are you all right? Where are you?"

"I heard you came to my building."

"Yeah, I did. Are you hurt? Do the bratva have you? What's going on?"

"Why don't *you* tell *me* what's going on?" she asks coldly, and I'm suddenly able to breathe a little better.

"Can we get together in person? No funny business, I

just want to explain everything to you. You definitely deserve the truth. Could we get coffee this afternoon?"

"This afternoon doesn't work." Natasha spins, her gaze seeking mine.

I frown and shake my head.

A crease appears between her brows.

I draw a line across my throat for her to cut the call.

"Listen, I really don't want to get together with you, Alex. You shot a friend of mine. You used me for your investigation. I'm not okay with any of that, and I really don't care to hear your side of the story. Have a nice life."

She hits *end*. "Happy?" She's mad at me, and I can't really blame her. I'm acting like a jealous twat when I have zero claim on this woman. And yet I still feel like throwing a teenager-sized tantrum.

I take the phone back. "Am I happy that douchebag is obviously still trying to use you?"

She winces at the words *use you,* and I remember the wound inflicted by her childhood friend. Dammit. I hate Alex all the more for pushing her soft spot.

"*Nyet.* No. Not at all. I'm not happy he's still breathing, frankly, and if he weren't a Fed, he wouldn't be."

Natasha blinks, color draining from her face. She takes a step back, her chest rising and falling quickly.

Blyad'. She's back to being terrified again. And I've confessed to being a killer.

"He could have *killed Nikolai,*" I tell her, pointing toward the bedroom where Nikolai is still suffering. "He is lucky I let him live." I don't know why I feel the need to defend my anger. The rational part of me knows I'm in the wrong here, but I just can't seem to find him. And it's all because of Natasha. What she does to me. To my sanity. "I still don't even know what he was looking for, but you know what I do know?"

She takes another step back. The rain stops like my tirade interrupted its flow. Only the smattering of drops falling from the trees patter against the roof and windows now.

"I know he never would've been at that game if you hadn't brought him. And I wouldn't have given you the address if you weren't *playing your fucking games* with me." I smack my palm against the window, and she recoils.

I already hate myself for being so cruel, but I can't seem to stop the rage and frustration from pouring out. Can't reel myself back in. Can't dial it back and apologize.

It takes her a couple of seconds to conquer the fear I just instilled in her, and when she does, it's a beautiful sight to see.

Natasha draws herself up, lips tightening, anger blazing in her bright eyes. Her skin changes from pale to flushed. and she tosses her ginger locks over one shoulder. "I can't change what happened." Her eyes swim with tears and fists clench at her sides. "If I could, I would. And you obviously can't get over it. So I think we'd better just keep our distance from each other until—" she breaks off, probably coming to the realization that she's not running this show. I set the rules. I decide if and when she gets to leave and what happens while she's here.

And that's probably what makes her run.

1 2

Natasha

I don't know where I'm going. All I know is I need some fresh air. I need to get away from Dima and his anger and blame. From my regrets and desires. From the constant churning and yearning Dima produces in me.

I throw open the back door and skid down the slick wooden steps from the deck to the rain-soaked earth. It's spongy and wet under my bare feet, mud sinking between my toes as I run.

"Natasha."

Damn him. He ignores me for hours on end, and the one time I need some space, he has to follow?

I keep running, heading into the thicket of trees, tears blinding me.

"Natasha, get back in the cabin!" Dima follows me.

I run faster.

"You really do love punishment don't you?" he shouts.

Oh, hell no. No, no, no, no, no. He doesn't get to throw that in my face. To shame me for the intimate acts we've shared.

I whirl and march back to him, slapping him across the face as hard as I can.

His blue eyes widen behind his black-framed glasses, dismay in the slackness of his mouth. "I guess I deserve that."

I turn again, intending to run, but he catches me around the waist. I scramble out of his grasp, but my feet slide in the mud, and I face-plant in a puddle.

"Oh, baby. Natasha, I'm sorry." Dima jogs up and crouches beside me.

For a moment, I don't move, praying the earth will open up and swallow me. When I feel Dima's hands on my shoulders, I try to scramble up. If I wanted to run from him before, the urge has quadrupled now.

"No, please." He catches me around the waist and drags me back, pulling us both to the ground, me cradled against his body in the mud.

"I'm sorry. I'm so sorry." He pushes my wet and mud-thick hair out of my face, his touch gentle. "None of this is your fault, Natasha. It's all on me." He cradles my cheek in his palm. "You're… you're special to me—I can't say why. And my attraction to you clouds my judgment." He plucks a wet lock of hair from my forehead and smooths it back. "I never should have given you the address for that game. I knew everything about it was wrong, but I got confused. And my mistake nearly killed Nikolai—" He shakes his head, closing his eyes as if in pain. "It's not the first time he's nearly died because of me."

It's all too raw and vulnerable. I want to bury my face and hide, but Dima's exposing his vulnerabilities, too, and it's impossible to look away.

Misery makes Dima's youthful face suddenly appear ancient. "He's the other half of me," he explains. "And all

I've done is drag him into danger. He's in the bratva because of me."

"He'll be okay," I promise. I'm not a doctor, but Nikolai seems like he's stable. Improving a little every day.

"I'm sorry you got mixed up in all this, Natasha. I'm sorry I blamed you. I've been an asshole. It's only because... I needed to push you away. It's hard for me to think straight when you're nearby. And I can't..." —he leans his forehead against mine and slowly shakes his head.

"Can't what?" I whisper.

"I'm not the guy for you, *amerikanka*. And you can't be mine."

Pain lances through my heart.

The urge to run again, to try to escape the ache of rejection hits me, but before I can struggle for sovereignty, Dima leans forward and brushes his lips against mine.

I go still. After all the things we've done, we've hardly kissed. He opens his lips, closes them around mine. His hand at my cheek slides around to cup the back of my head, and he holds me steady as he deepens the kiss, firming his lips against mine, tasting me, then sweeping his tongue into my mouth.

I loop my arm behind his neck and kiss him back. Nothing has ever felt so good—this messy, vulnerable meeting of lips, mating of mouths in the middle of a puddle after a rainstorm. My body comes alive, every nerve-ending responding to the intensity of his kiss. My nipples harden under my tight, wet t-shirt, I go slick between my legs.

I shift position to straddle his waist, and then he pushes me back into the mud.

"Natasha." It's a lament. Like he's broken. Like he's sorry.

Whether he's sorry for hurting me or sorry for what we're about to do, I can't be sure.

He kisses along my jaw, sucks at my neck. "I want you," he rasps, sounding breathless.

"I want you, too," I murmur.

He unbuttons his jeans and frees his length, and then he pushes into me, my panties and the boxer shorts easily shoved down. My back sinks into the soft mud as he pins my wrists beside my head and slowly, gently rocks, holding my gaze as if we're performing some sacred ritual that requires his utmost concentration.

"You're so beautiful," he murmurs. "You can't possibly know how beautiful you are to me."

His words enter me, swirling and spiraling up my center core, received like broken fragments of his withheld love. A few more pieces I will cling to and save for later, for those moments when I try to rearrange and fit them together, trying to make it real. Make it whole.

I love you, Dima.

Those are the words in my head that I want to say, but I hold them back.

He's already said I'm not for him, and he can't be for me.

Is it possible to love someone who can't be for you?

Yes! my tattered heart screams. It may not be logical, but it's true. I've always felt something for Dima, just as he's always felt something for me.

There's a rightness when I'm with him. A sense that I know him, even though I don't. And even after all his rejections, I'm still here, taking whatever he's willing to give, waiting for the moment when he's ready to give more.

"Natasha." He dips his head and nuzzles into my neck, all the while moving in a steady rhythm inside me. "You are summer rain and the sun that shines afterward." He nips my ear. "You are everything kind and pure in my world. And I've been jaded for such a long time."

He kisses along my collarbone. "I would help you with my fingers, but they're covered in mud," he murmurs like he's telling me a secret he doesn't want the trees to hear.

I laugh. "I'll come if you go harder."

Dima's eyes warm. His smile is soft and indulgent. "My biggest surprise with you," he says, releasing my wrists and bracing his hands on the ground beside my head to thrust deeper.

"What?"

"That you like it rough. I never would have guessed."

"Me neither," I admit, my eyes already rolling back in my head as he increases the intensity of his strokes, slamming in harder and deeper, but still at a slow, measured pace.

The pressure in me grows, building and coiling tighter until Dima murmurs, "Are you close?"

I nod, my gaze locked on his. He doesn't blink, doesn't look away. He pins me with that beautiful blue stare and drills into me, faster, harder, until need makes his movements jerky, his mouth open.

"Natasha!" he gasps.

"I'm coming!" My muscles tighten around his thick member, and he thrusts even harder and faster, pumping to his finish while I come and come beneath him.

When it's over, when I open my eyes—I don't know when I closed them—I find he's still staring down at me with that same crazy intensity.

"Dima."

I don't know why it feels like our first time.

It feels like my first time, ever.

Maybe because sex has never felt so intimate and

shared. It wasn't beautiful or romantic or hot. I didn't have sexy lingerie on. He didn't show me his expert moves.

We broke apart in the mud, and then we put each other back together, one thrust at a time, until we were nearly whole again. Whole, but rearranged, as if some of my broken parts were glued to his and his to mine.

He lowers his head slowly and presses a kiss to my forehead. "Let's get you out of the mud." His voice is kindness and whispers. He slips out of me and straightens the panties and boxer shorts. "Come here, *rodnaya*." He tugs me off the ground and up into his arms, and for a moment, he just holds me.

Sunshine filters through the pine trees, lighting up the water droplets and making the forest sparkle.

He kisses the top of my head, loops an arm around me, and steers me back into the cabin.

There's a sadness to him—like he'd been holding all that anger in place between us before, and now that it's fallen away, he mourns something.

Or some*one*.

Maybe he regrets breaking his promise to her.

Has he chosen me? Or was this another one of his mistakes?

I can't bring myself to ask. It feels too nice to have his arm protectively around me. To have him whispering sweet things to me. To ride the post-orgasmic bliss as far as it will take us.

He takes my hand when we get inside and leads me to my bathroom upstairs where he peels my soaked t-shirt from my body, then crouches down to lower my panties and his boxers, tugging them off my ankles.

I stand there, soaking up his attention, letting it seep into all the cracks and crevices he split open these past few days.

He turns on the water in the shower and helps me in, then strips out of his clothes and joins me. Dirt, pine needles, and tiny leaves turn the water at my feet into mud soup. Dima's smile is soft as he helps clean the dirt from my forehead and my hair. He picks up the bar of soap and runs his hands over me. It's sensual but not sexual. He has a semi, but I don't think he's seducing me.

It's more like… he's asking forgiveness.

Making it up to me.

There's an ease between us. Like neither of us want anything from the other; we're just content to be together. To exist in the same energy. To commune, I guess.

I shampoo my hair while he soaps his body. We change places, so he can rinse.

"Are you okay?" he asks softly when he opens his eyes and finds me watching.

I was admiring how beautiful he is, in awe to find myself feeling so close to him. I nod.

"There's a frozen pizza I could put in the oven for dinner."

I smile. It's so comfortable and familiar. So ordinary. Like we're long-time live-in lovers instead of neighbors with no benefits. A captive and her captor. "That sounds nice."

"You finished?" he asks, hand on the water nozzle. When I nod, he turns off the shower and pulls open the curtain. He grabs the closest towel and hands it to me, like a gentleman.

I wrap it around myself and stare at the filthy clothes on the floor. "Looks like I'm back to wearing the damn dress."

"My torture," he murmurs, as he dries his body in swift, efficient movements. His admission sends fluffy cotton candy clouds of pleasure floating through me.

Except I still sense the sadness in him. Weariness. Defeat. Or am I misinterpreting contrition? He wraps the towel around his waist and picks up the heap of our muddy clothes. "I'll get these washed and turn the oven on."

I stare after him, trying not to spin out on domestic chore porn.

Things have changed between us, yes. But as sweet as Dima's being, I don't think he's happy about the change.

He's just not angry anymore.

13

Dima

I go down the stairs and turn on the oven, then lean my ass against the counter and stare at the wall. What am I doing?

What in *the hell* am I doing?

I can't do this with Natasha.

And yet… I had no choice. Hanging her out to dry would've been unconscionable. I've already been crueler to her than I can face.

Seeing her broken and knowing I was the one who broke her? That gutted me.

I'll have to live with that shit until the day I die.

So yeah, I don't see any other way around this. I need to put her back together. Try to heal the wounds I've inflicted before I set her free.

The guilt over the way I've treated Natasha mingles with the guilt I feel over breaking my vow to Alyona.

I'm still yours, I promise her. *I'll always be yours.*

Strange how, despite my gnawing guilt, the bond with Alyona feels stronger than usual. Maybe it's because my memories of her have come so near the surface. Being intimate with someone again brings it all back. What it was like the first time. How we learned each other's bodies. How I would've died if it meant she could've lived out her youth.

I don't compare Natasha—they are totally different people. I'm a totally different person with her than I was with Alyona.

I don't want them to blur together for me. Not at all. It's important to me that I preserve every memory of Alyona.

The oven beeps, and I realize I haven't moved since I turned it on.

I pull the frozen pizza from the freezer, unbox it and throw it on the rack, set my phone timer for 16 minutes, and then I take our dirty clothes to the washing machine and throw them in on the shortest cycle possible. Having the two of us running around here naked is not going to work for me.

When I pop my head into the master bedroom, I find Nikolai awake.

"I'm hungry," he says.

"Good. I'll heat up some soup."

He groans. "I smell pizza."

I wince. "Sorry, the doctor said only soups or soft foods for now." We had a telecall with Taylor this morning to check in. "You want a laptop in here, so you can watch movies or something?"

"*Da.*"

I go and get him the laptop, and as I set it up, he says, "You should keep her."

My fingers stall over the keys. Alyona's ring catches the light, winking at me. "I can't."

"You can. It's allowed, Dima. Whatever rule you made

for yourself at seventeen can be changed. Just like Ravil changes bratva rules. The ones that used to mean death if we broke them."

"*Don't*," I say firmly, something shuddering and cracking inside me. "Leave it alone." I don't look at him like I have to keep my pain in, keep it to myself.

"It's allowed," Nikolai repeats, but his voice carries no fight.

I leave him with the laptop and walk away, my body suddenly feeling a million years old.

Natasha comes downstairs, her fresh-faced beauty even more excruciating because she's dressed in a towel.

She steps into the kitchen, fidgeting with the ends of the terrycloth above her left breast. "May I help with anything?"

"*Nyet, amerikanka.* See if you can find a movie on the television." I speak gently, but I desperately need some distance between us.

She curls up on the L-shaped leather sofa and pulls a plush blanket around her, which alleviates some of my tension. I slide the pizza out and cut a small piece for Nikolai, bringing it to him first. Then I pile the rest on one plate for Natasha and I to share. I bring a roll of paper towels into the living room and sit down beside her to share.

"What are you in the mood for?" She spins through Netflix as fast as I would, sliding over the shows.

"You pick," I tell her. At the penthouse, I might throw down with Sasha, making a big fuss over not watching chick-flicks, but that's all for play. Right now, I just want Natasha to be soothed. So whatever she wants to watch is fine with me.

She turns those big green eyes on me for a moment, then scrolls even faster. "Um… I can't." She bites her lip, looking adorable. "I don't know what you like."

"Don't pick for me, pick for you." I gesture at her with a slice of pizza. It tastes as cardboardy as the box it was in.

She's obviously still troubled by my answer because a crease appears between her brows as she scrolls down. She picks comedies, then slides through them. "*Easy A*?"

"Never seen it."

She hits play, and we eat and watch in silence.

Of course, it's a movie about sex. With an adorable redhead as the heroine.

And I'm sitting beside Natasha, who is naked under that blanket.

But at least I'm not suffering from that blinding need to claim her like I was before. I'm not gnashing my teeth, ready to lash out because I can barely control myself. Something about taking her out there in the mud—the honesty behind it, maybe—loosened that noose. I admitted I wanted her, and I took her.

It was wrong, but it was also right.

And now I need to clean up the mess I made.

When the movie ends, I hit pause on the credits. "Natasha…"

She turns, her lovely face open and inquisitive. She has no makeup here, but she looks no different—her beauty is a natural one that doesn't require much enhancement.

She's close enough that I can smell the scent of her shampoo, feel the heat of her body beside mine.

I twitch the blanket farther up her bare shoulder. "You're okay?"

She studies me. "I'm okay. Are you?"

I shake my head. "Not really, no." I pick up her hand and hold it, staring down at her slender, pale fingers. The short, clean nails which had been polished in pale ballet pink, but are now half-chipped off. "I won't call it a mistake. Only making you cry—that was unforgivable." I close my eyes and shake my head.

Her fingers close around mine. I readjust, untangling our fingers and holding her hand in both mine, stroking down each of her digits and giving it a little twist on the end, like she does when she's massaging me.

One corner of her mouth tips up as she must recognize her own move. "That feels good," she says softly.

I keep working. "These hands are so small for how much pressure you put through them. I can't believe how hard you can dig with them."

The smile appears at both corners now. "Sometimes I use my elbow."

I raise my brows, surprised. "Ah? I didn't know. Huh." I pick up her other hand and give it the same treatment. "I care about you," I admit. "And I'm obviously very attracted to you. But…"

"You can't have a relationship," she finishes for me. I see a flicker of hurt before she hides it, and it makes me want to do everything in my power to fix it.

Except I can't.

"Right. I don't want to hurt you—I mean, I know I already have—but I don't want to hurt you more."

"It's okay," she says softly. Her eyes tear up, but she blinks it back. "Can we, um, can we be friends?"

I wrap her hand up in both of mine and squeeze. "We *are* friends," I promise. "I know I haven't been a good one, but I've always considered you a friend."

Her nod is earnest. There's a tremble in her lips, but she hides it by tugging the blanket up over her chin.

"So no more sex. I'm going to be the girl and say it's too confusing for me."

She gives a watery laugh. "No more sex." She slumps

back against the couch, her head dropping to the fluffy cushion. "This sucks."

Understatement. And all my fault.

"I agree. I'm sorry." I reach out and stroke my hand over the back of her head.

"Is a cuddle out of bounds?"

"A… cuddle?" A rusty laugh comes from my throat as my chest squeezes. "You need a little sugar?"

She nods, leaning into me as I lift my arm to loop around her. She rests her head against my shoulder and molds to my side, sweetness and summer and angel wings wrapped into one.

I find another movie and turn it on, propping my feet on the coffee table. Her legs tangle over the top of mine, and her breath evens.

When I'm sure she's asleep, I stroke her face and kiss the top of her head. And then I don't move a muscle, even when I remember the laundry in the washer. Not when I decide I have to pee and should really check on Nikolai.

I don't move because Natasha needed this cuddle, and I'll be damned if I'm going to wake her up and take it away.

~

Natasha

I jerk awake with a gasp.

No, that wasn't my gasp. I lift my head in the dim light to peer at Dima. We're still on the sofa, our bodies intertwined. I must've fallen asleep during the last movie, which is obviously over now because the television is off.

"*Izvinyayus'*," Dima mutters an apology, and I realize it was a sharp movement from him that woke me.

"Did you have a bad dream?"

"*Da.*" He hasn't switched to English yet. I understand Russian perfectly. I can speak it perfectly, too, once I'm in the mode, but I prefer English. After Pamela's in-school rejection, I made a choice. Dima was right, I Americanized myself completely.

I press my hand over his heart, not surprised when I find it racing. "What was it?"

"You and Nikolai and A—" He breaks off, shaking his head. "Just… people I care about dying. Because of me."

"What happened to Nikolai wasn't your fault," I tell him, pulling away to sit up straighter.

His gaze drops to my left breast, which has come out from the blanket. A muscle jumps in his jaw, and he scoots away from me.

"No, it was Alex's fault, and I will make him pay."

He's back to being grumpy-Dima, and it all becomes perfectly clear now. His anger toward me was a redirection of his own guilt. He's suffering over this—he told me that outside in that puddle.

It's not the first time he's nearly died because of me.

"What if it all just… was? What if it's nobody's fault—just a series of events?"

Dima scoffs.

"I mean, we assign meaning to things. Death is bad. Birth is good. But is that really true? If no one ever died, the planet wouldn't survive. Leaving Russia was bad, trying to integrate into school was bad, but was it really? I don't regret who I am today. What if there was no right or wrong. No good or bad. No one to blame."

Dima scrubs his hand over his face.

"I'm sorry Nikolai's suffering, but… I'm not sorry I had this time here with you—even the bad parts." I shrug. "It is what it is."

Dima meets my gaze and holds it. "You're wise for your age."

"I just want you to be free," I whisper hoarsely, and we both know I'm talking about more than his guilt over Nikolai.

Before he can shut me down, I stand, pulling the blanket up to my armpits. The towel I was originally wearing tangles around my legs and falls. "*Spokoynoy nochi.*" I say good night as I walk away.

"*Spokoynoy nochi.*" His answer is soft and full of regret.

14

Dima

"I just checked on Nikolai, and he's fine. Bingeing Netflix. Want to go for a walk?" Natasha leans a hip against the office door frame, looking like sunshine itself. Yesterday Ravil sent Adrian here with clothes and necessities for both of us and more groceries, so at least she's not driving me insane in that tiny t-shirt and my boxers.

Not that the halter top and short-shorts are any better.

I had Adrian bring her expensive gourmet chocolate bars, too, which made her look at me in a way that seared my insides.

It's been two days of us being friends, which is the best and worst thing ever.

For one thing, it's way too easy. Too comfortable. Almost like we shot past the tearing our clothes off around each other straight into the sweetest long-term marriage minus the sex.

She's sweet as pie, doing things like making pancakes and coffee. She makes jokes and dazzles me with her quick, easy smile. She stands behind me at the computer and massages my neck with those magic fingers of hers. I had to refuse her offer for a full massage, knowing we'd be right back in the clothes-tearing territory.

I'm not even sure how I keep from going there now, except by holding onto the pain and defeat I'd felt after I let myself have her out in the mud. I keep that bite of sadness with me everywhere. Like a talisman I rub every time my gaze starts to wander over her luscious body.

Say no. Say no.

I want to do the right thing. I could tell her to go on her own. I stopped acting like her warden after our roll in the mud.

But resisting her doesn't feel like the right thing anymore, either.

So I push back from the office chair and stand. I might as well take a break. I'm still no closer to figuring out what the FBI is after, nor what secret Alex holds, although I feel certain there's more to him than I know. Is it about Natasha? Or the bratva? That's the part I can't figure out.

I shove my feet into my shoes.

"I'm so happy to have my sneakers here," Natasha says as she pulls on her red Chucks.

"I'll bet." I touch her back as I reach past her to open the back door. "Heels really aren't you, are they?"

Her laugh is chagrined, and she ducks her head. "No."

I stop myself from asking if she'd worn them for me, as well.

Outside, the light has taken on the first color changes of sunset—an orange swath cutting across the top layer of the trees. We follow the path from the cabin that leads to the road.

It feels so natural to take her hand—so natural that I yank my fingers away the moment they brush hers, shocked at the instinct.

Friends.

Friends.

It's my new mantra. The one I can't seem to get my entire being on board with.

"How did you end up in the bratva?" Her question sounds so innocent; she has no idea how charged it is for me.

She catches my frown and her forehead crinkles. "I'm sorry—I'm probably not allowed to ask that."

Hating her to be sorry, I try to cover it. "You're not wearing a wire, are you? Do I need to search you again?"

A blush spreads across her neck, pooling in the hollow of her neck and dipping into the cleavage that's so nicely framed by her turquoise print halter. "There's a mud puddle back there you might use." She jerks a thumb behind us, and I can't stop my reluctant smile.

This is exactly what's been so excruciating. There's no awkwardness about what's happened. She's so fucking precious it bruises my heart.

"Don't tempt me," I mutter.

At least it's all out in the open now. I can own my attraction, and we've agreed it can't be acted on.

It's against the rules to talk about any bratva business with anyone outside the brotherhood, and yet I know she's asking because of what I'd confessed back there in that puddle. That Nikolai was in the bratva because of me.

"I borrowed money for...someone who needed it. I was trying to save a life." I slide a glance her way. The warm hues of sunset pick up the red and copper in her hair, making it shimmer and glow in a halo around her.

You're beautiful.

I manage not to say it out loud.

She is. Heart-achingly beautiful.

"I sold my soul."

"And what about Nikolai?"

"I sold his, too." I spot a large boulder and scramble up it, sitting on the top with my arms draped around my knees. Natasha follows.

We sit in silence for a few moments. "I don't believe you."

My laugh is dark and bitter. "No? Why not?"

"You wouldn't do that. He chose to come with you, right?"

A shudder of some unknown emotion runs through me. Guilt? Shame? The darkness of those early days, those early years washes over me like a dark bloodstain. One that will never come off, no matter how light or easy our existence in Ravil's cell may seem in comparison.

"He chose." The guilt of it nearly suffocates me. "He came with me when I borrowed the money. He was part of it from the beginning. He did it all for me."

"Why is that so wrong?" Her voice is so soft it can't be registered as a challenge. It's like her questions the other night, after the mud sex. *What if it was no one's fault?*

But I don't know how to see things if not through the lens and weight of my own guilt.

"It's wrong because we died that night."

Natasha goes still, waiting for more.

I work to swallow and fail. This is not a story I've ever told. Nikolai and I don't talk about it. The rest of the brotherhood wouldn't ask—they have their own stories to hold.

"The bratva…" My voice sounds rusty. "We swear an oath to the brotherhood and one part is to cut ties with all other family. That way no one ever has leverage over you, and your ties are only to your brothers."

Natasha is quick to follow. "Your family thinks you both are dead."

I nod. "*Da.*" For a moment, I can't speak, the shame and horror of what we put our mother through ripping me to shreds. And then I start talking. "We were seventeen. It was just our mom—our dad walked out when we were six. We were all she had." My throat tightens around a well of pain.

Natasha covers her mouth, her eyes swimming with the tears I haven't produced. Like she's my surrogate heart, willing to emote what I've held in all these years.

"She thinks we died in a car crash—our car went into an icy river, and no bodies were ever found."

"Oh God," Natasha whispers.

I nod, grateful she understands the magnitude of it all. How horrible a man I truly am.

"Can you *imagine* how much she must have suffered?" My voice breaks.

"No." A tear tracks down Natasha's cheek. She brushes it away with the back of her hand. "That's awful, Dima. I can tell it's killing you."

Killing me.

I never thought of it that way. I thought of it as something in the past. A metaphoric death for both Nikolai and I. The day we entered a life of violence and crime. I didn't think of it as something that continued to kill me, but she's right. It's like a cancer eating a hole in my gut, day by day.

Getting worse as each year passes instead of fading away.

Is Alyona's death the same? That pain certainly hasn't eased. Maybe because it's all tied into the same event. The same time period. I sold my soul for Alyona, broke my mother's heart and forced my brother into a life of crime, and it never did a bit of good. I couldn't save Alyona. I just wished I'd died with her.

And, in a way, I had.

It doesn't take a psychiatrist to point out that I'm hardly in the world of the living. I spend my hours behind a screen because I don't want to interact with anyone in real life. Even my brothers in the penthouse.

I trace my fingertip over the lichen on the boulder. "We've taken care of our mom. I, uh, arranged early retirement, so she gets a healthy pension. And she... wins quite a few contests. Home makeovers and clothing sprees."

Natasha's smile is sad. "That's sweet. At least you can still take care of her from afar."

Not really, but Natasha calling it sweet is a kindness to me.

We stare into the trees for a few moments, and then Natasha leans her forehead on my shoulder and kisses my biceps. I kiss the top of her head.

We're sweet.

And it doesn't feel wrong. This tenderness between us never feels wrong.

"But Ravil has a family. And Maxim has Sasha. And Oleg has Story." Natasha's up to speed quickly again.

"*Da.* Ravil broke the code with Lucy and their baby Benjamin. Then Maxim's marriage was ordered by the *pakhan* back in Moscow, by Sasha's father." I shrug. "So once they'd broken it, the rules loosened for all of us."

"So... do you think you could... reach out to your mom now? Maybe tell her you and Nikolai are alive? Visit her?"

Bile rises up my throat. I shake my head. "You think she could forgive the pain we brought her? That she could accept what we've become? *Nyet.* Better to let her believe we are dead."

"I...have to disagree. I think she'd be overjoyed to know you're both alive. You may not be proud of what happened in the past, but I think she could see beyond it. I mean, I don't know what you've done—and I don't want to know—" she adds quickly, "but no matter what it is, I know you're both good men."

"How do you know this thing, Natasha?"

"I just know." I hear that note of stubbornness in her voice, and it makes a smile tug at my lips.

Natasha gasps, lifting her head and gripping my forearm.

Every muscle in my body tenses, the need to protect her a white-hot scream, but then I see what she does.

A doe.

A beautiful, big-eyed doe staring straight at us.

Natasha's fingers tighten on my forearm to convey her excitement. "Dima," she breathes, barely making a sound.

We hold perfectly still, watching our forest friend as she dips her head and bites a tuft of sweet grass. When she lifts her head again, she slowly chews it, pinning us again with her beautiful gaze.

"I love her," Natasha whispers. "I love her so much."

It's a funny thing to say. Not that she loves seeing a deer, but she loves the doe. The one she's only known for thirty seconds.

This is what makes Natasha special. Miraculous. One of a kind.

Every moment that passes it feels like she's pulling me into the world of the living—falling in love with animals. Calling my actions sweet.

None of that feels wrong.

Our doe turns and majestically walks into the forest, and only when she's out of sight do we turn and look at each other.

"That was amazing," Natasha sighs, a little smile playing around her lips.

I kiss her forehead. "You're amazing."

I'm starting to wonder if she could be right—that Nikolai getting shot wasn't the most horrible thing that's ever happened.

Even though I don't get to keep Natasha, I get this.

I had this moment with her.

And it feels like a gift.

It's not enough, but I'll take it.

We won't be here much longer. Dr. Taylor, the vet, said Nikolai can start to get up and move around now when he wants, and Natasha took his IV out today. Another day or two is all I have with her.

Another day or two of exquisite torture.

And then maybe I can sleep at night without fucking my fist for an hour to stop thinking about her.

Maybe we can stay friends until she leaves for naturopathy school.

But no. Even as I think it, I know I've pushed this thing between us way farther than it should go. Even though I've been honest about not being available for a relationship, we're developing one.

And to let it go on would be a cruelty to both of us.

15

Dima

    I'm in the hot tub with Natasha. Just as friends. We're in the hot tub, watching a movie together, her legs tangled over mine, her head leaning on my shoulder.

    It's a horror movie, and she cuddles closer and closer until she's on my lap, her soft wet ass nesting over my junk. And then it's not the hot tub anymore, it's the couch, and I have my hand between her legs, running my middle finger along her juicy slit. She starts moaning and arching, and I penetrate her… but then I hear Alyona's voice. She's in the cabin—in my room talking to Nikolai.

    I need to get Natasha off my lap, except I can't seem to move her. I keep trying, keep remembering I need to stop touching her, need to push her off my lap, and get up, but I can never seem to get up.

                    ~

I WAKE with my heart racing and a boner the size of the Spasskaya Tower. Guilt coats the inside of my mouth, turns my stomach sour.

    Beside me, Nikolai groans as he lurches to his feet to go

to the bathroom on his own. Dr. Taylor gave him the go-ahead to get vertical again, if he's feeling it.

"Need help?" I ask in Russian.

"*Nyet.*" He hobbles slowly, killing me with his sharp breaths, but I'm not going to hover. Nikolai's not a baby, and he doesn't want my sympathy.

My dream made me crabby as hell. I don't need Carl Jung to interpret it for me. All my dreams since I got here have been pretty fucking obvious. My sins mashed up and rearranged for me to review, to remember what an utter piece of shit I am.

I can't touch Natasha again. Not a chaste kiss. Not a cuddle. Nothing.

No more sunset walks in the forest. No watching movies together on the couch at night.

I need some fucking distance.

In fact, I'll call Ravil today to ask if he's okay with us coming back to the Kremlin. I don't think we need to hide out anymore—it's been six days, and nothing's happened with Alex, other than his visit to the Kremlin, which seemed more off-the-job than FBI sanctioned. Seems like he would've come with a partner if it was official FBI business.

Not that I'm an expert on FBI procedures. I did hack in and download a training manual, though. Heh.

I skip breakfast and go straight to my computer. Lucy got back to me with her rewrites on Natasha's admission essay, which are brilliant. I go to work internet time traveling to make it look like everything was submitted to all the schools last fall or winter.

It takes me all morning, and I'm surly with Natasha when she asks if I want breakfast because I don't want her coming in.

Then I'm surly when I'm done because this is almost

the end. We need to get out of this cabin, and then she's going away for four years. It's what needs to happen, but I still feel like punching a wall.

The video chat rings on my laptop, and I answer the call from Ravil. He's in his office, Maxim sitting beside him.

"How is Nikolai?" he asks.

"Good. He's moving around a little and eating soft foods. I think we could come back to the Kremlin if you think it's safe."

"Excellent. Is he awake now?"

"Probably. He's awake more often lately."

"Let me see him."

I stand and unplug my laptop, walking to the bedroom. I sit beside Nikolai on the bed, so Ravil can see both of us.

"Nikolai. You look like shit," Maxim says.

"I look prettier than you any day," he shoots back.

"How are you feeling?" Ravil asks.

"Like a rhino trampled me," Nikolai says. "Ready to get out of this damn bed."

"Good. As soon as you feel up for the drive, you can come back," Ravil says. "We've had no more visits from Alex." He directs this news to me. "He never produced a search warrant or returned."

"Part of me thinks he's off the rails with the FBI," Maxim says. "My theory is that he has a personal interest in us or else in Natasha. Something about the way he showed up here alone and then left with his tail tucked doesn't feel by-the-FBI-book to me."

"I'd love to know what report he filed after that game. Have you had any luck hacking the FBI?" Maxim asks.

I grumble in frustration. "Not really. I haven't found case files—that's what we really need here."

"You say he wanted to get together with Natasha to explain?"

I nod. "Yes. He texted a few times and mentioned it again when she called him."

"Have her take him up on it when you get back. He offered. I'd love to know his explanation."

White noise fills my ears.

Cold prickles flush over my skin.

Oh, hell no. She's not going out with him again.

"Absolutely not," I say, even though defying my *pakhan* is idiotic.

Ravil raises his brows in warning.

Maxim lowers his. "Are you worried about her safety? An FBI agent isn't going to hurt an innocent woman." He folds his arms over his chest. "Or are you worried she's actually part of this?"

I want to punch the laptop in, but Nikolai answers for me. "She's not part of it." He says it with total confidence and clarity.

"Then there's nothing to fear. If nothing else, it will show us if our boy Alex is off the rails because of his feelings for her."

I grind my molars, but there's nothing else I can say. I don't want her near him because I'm a jealous fuck, and that's not a valid reason to defy Ravil. There is no defiance of your *pakhan* in the bratva. Not unless you want to face torture at the blades of all your brothers. Not that I've seen that happen under Ravil's rule.

"Arrange it, Dima," Ravil orders. "As soon as you three are back in town. I don't like this cloud hanging over us."

I scowl but force myself to nod, showing my acquiescence.

Nikolai also nods.

"Take care of yourself, Nikolai," Ravil says. "I'm

looking forward to having you both back. Things are quiet around here with Pavel gone and now you two."

As if to contradict his father, the sound of Benjamin's happy shriek suddenly comes across the screen.

Ravil's normally inscrutable mask transforms into a broad smile. "There you are. Are you crawling in to visit your papa?"

The baby's coos grow closer, and Maxim leans over and reappears with Benjamin. At nine months, the baby is sturdy and plump, with big thunder thighs and a buddha belly although learning to crawl recently seems to be slimming him down.

"Come here, big boy." Ravil takes the child and holds him in the air, blowing a raspberry on his bare belly.

Benjamin giggles.

"Text me when you leave the cabin," Ravil instructs. "And get that meeting with Alex arranged today."

"*Da, pakhan*," I murmur, ending the call.

Der'mo. Setting Natasha up on a date with Alex is the last thing I want to do now or ever.

16

Natasha

I come inside from sunbathing on the deck in the late afternoon and head up the stairs.

Dima's been a dick all day—he's back to snarls and not speaking to me. I can't figure out what's going on, and I'm sick of the whiplash I'm getting from this guy.

Honestly, his being mean again makes it easier.

We were getting too close. Heartbreakingly close. I could really fall for this guy.

Who am I kidding? I *have* fallen for him. And as much as I love how comfortable we are together—this friendship thing—I want the full package. And I've been clinging to the hope that with a little patience, he'll realize he wants it, too.

But the closer we get, the more melancholy it seems to make him. His fingers are always on that little ring— twisting it around his pinky with an ocean of pain in his eyes.

"Where have you been?" He appears in the doorway to my room now. I didn't hear him come up the stairs.

"I was right outside on the deck. What's up?"

He hands me my phone. "You need to call Alex."

"What?"

Anger radiates from Dima, and I can't, for the life of me, figure out what his problem could be.

He makes an impatient motion with his hand through the air. "You need to make date with him." His accent is thicker with his irritation.

"No." I don't really know what I did wrong here, but I'm not going to let him push me around. My emotions are too raw from a week of the Dima rollercoaster.

"Ravil's orders." His lips screw together in a grim line.

Ah. It dawns on me why he's mad. He's just the messenger. And he doesn't like the message. He may not want a relationship with me, but that doesn't mean he wants me going out with Alex.

Well, he doesn't need to worry. I'm not dating Alex—ever again. Even if he hadn't shot Nikolai, I won't forgive him for making a fool out of me.

"No." I make my voice even but firm. "I'm not going out with Alex."

"Natasha." Dima takes a warning step toward me. There's a predatory threat to his movement that unfortunately turns me on.

The energy of our explosive punishment-and-reward play rekindles, sending a bold spike of heat straight to my core.

Dima catches my wrist. "Sorry, *amerikanka*. I don't like it, either. Not one bit. But it's not up to you or me. We need to know more about Alex's motivation and target, and he offered to get together with you to explain. So now you have to go."

I shake my head. "I don't have to." I'm feeling stubborn. More importantly, I'm testing boundaries here. Dima doesn't want me to go, either. Will he really push me into this?

Dima's brows dip. He tightens his hold on my wrist, walking me backward until my butt hits the wall. "You do, Natasha. It's not up for discussion."

"You can't make me," I dare. I shouldn't push, but I crave his touch again. Relish the moments when he's caved to his desires for me.

It doesn't work. Instead of goading him, Dima appears genuinely troubled.

I regret pushing him until he counters with, "I can make you do anything."

My nipples harden to tight points. *Please?*

"Natasha, I don't want to threaten you." I can hear the honesty in Dima's words, almost like it makes him sick to think of putting the pressure on me.

Which must mean he's refusing to engage sexually, the way he "handled" me before.

Disappointment churns in my stomach.

Maybe it really is all over.

I didn't want to accept the friendship thing. I kept thinking he'd see that we have something together and realize that choosing a living, breathing woman is better than hanging onto a ghost.

But apparently, I was wrong.

"Why are you doing this?" He's practically pleading for my cooperation. That's how much he doesn't want to take me in hand. "This isn't you."

He's right, of course. I'm agreeable, sweet Natasha who does what's expected of her to keep the peace above all else. Always seeking acceptance and approval.

"I like it when you're mad," I tell him. It's my last-ditch effort to get somewhere with him.

It works. His eyes darken, brows shoot to his hairline.

The air between us charges, and I sense every ounce of the friendship we were cultivating drain. We're back to something else. Opponents in a sex war.

The one where blood is drawn at the same time satisfaction is delivered.

He rips my shirt off over my head in a single, swift motion. Punishment *is on.*

Tingles race down my arms as he takes in my black lace bra.

"Is that right?"

I press myself against the wall, not that I'm scared. Well, I'm a little scared. Thrilled is more like it. I give him a nod.

"You want me to put you on your hands and knees and spank that ass red?" He turns me around, facing away from him, and unhooks the bra, pushing the straps down my arms until it falls to the floor. He cups both my breasts, pinching my nipples hard. "Pull down your shorts." His voice is rusty.

I unbutton my jean shorts, and they drop to the floor, too. My panties match the bra—black lace.

That's the moment Dima must realize how I got a matching set of sexy underwear—Adrian had brought them yesterday with our other things.

"Adrian went through your drawers," he chokes.

I look over my shoulder to check the level of rage on his face. My tummy flutters. I love seeing him mad—it's when I get a glimpse of his level of passion for me. I hold his jealousy close to my chest as proof of what I mean to him.

His hand slaps down on my ass. "I'm going to kill him."

I hide my smile.

"Come here, pretty girl." He takes my waist with both

hands and pulls me away from the wall, then walks me to the bed. "On your hands and knees."

My pulse races as I crawl onto the mattress and assume the position.

Dima slaps my ass a few times. "You like me mad?"

I make a little sound—not really a whimper. More like a sex sound. The kind that means *more.*

"Hmm?" He delivers a few more spanks then strokes his hand over my right cheek. "If Adrian thought of you in these panties, I will smash his face in," he mutters, more to himself than to me.

I smother a giggle, but Dima catches it. "You think that's funny?" He delivers a flurry of slaps, warming the lower half of my ass. "No!" I squeal when it gets intense, and he immediately stops and rubs away the sting. "He said Nadia packed my things," I admit. Nadia is Adrian's sister.

"I don't want to send you on a date with that cock-sucker Alex," he growls. "You think I would ask if I didn't have to?"

I don't want to think about Alex. I don't want Dima bringing him up between us now, ruining the moment.

He gives my ass another hard slap. "You can't refuse Ravil on this."

I remain still, panting slightly, incredibly aroused.

He grips my hair and tugs my head back. "Natasha." His voice is firm, demanding an answer.

"I'll do it," I say.

Dima relaxes his grip on my hair but keeps it wound around his fist.

"On one condition." My heart pounds in my ears, at my wrists, in my temples.

He releases my hair completely and delivers three hard

spanks. "You're not making the conditions here, *amerikanka*."

I look over my shoulder at him. "I think I am." I no longer believe anything terrible will happen to me. Dima wouldn't let it happen, and Ravil gave him responsibility for me. Which means I have the chips to bargain with.

Dima's eyes narrow. "What is your condition?"

I've never felt so vulnerable, and it has nothing to do with the position I'm in. It's what I'm about to ask. "Tell me why you can't be with me. Because I know we both feel something."

Dima sucks in a breath, then his jaw hardens. "No." There's no missing the note of stubbornness in his voice. "That story is not for you, Natasha. I'm not for you."

I fight back the stab of rejection, the flush of shame that climbs up my throat. But no, he didn't deny what's between us. He just wants to hang onto his ghost. I still think we're worth fighting for. "Then I'm not going out with Alex," I tell him.

His face darkens. "You think you will win this battle with me?"

"Yes."

Dima won't hurt me. I'm sure of it. He has feelings for me, whether he'll admit them or not.

He rips my panties down my legs and grabs my ankles, pulling me toward him until I slide to my belly. He disappears for a moment, stooping down, and when he rises, he has my bra, which he uses to tie my hands behind my back. I'm gushing arousal, so hot and ready for him. I've never been tied up before, but I now understand the appeal. The sense of being at his mercy amplifies everything—my desire, my need for him, the heat flooding my body.

He dips his fingers between my legs and strokes over

my dewy petals. It feels so good to have his touch where I needed it so badly. I tip my pelvis back and moan.

"Even pleasure can be a torture, Natasha." His voice is smoky velvet. He slides his fingers inside me at the same time his thumb traces down the cleft of my ass until it reaches my anus.

I moan and hump the bed. I'm already so wound up, and being bound and spread for him just makes the whole experience hotter.

"You think I won't fuck this cute little ass?"

I undulate my hips to take his fingers deeper. I'm freaked out about anal, but not enough to not want it. I already know from what he did to me downstairs on the kitchen counter how incredible it feels. How much I liked anal play.

I'm feverish, rubbing my bare breasts over the bedcovers, arching and rolling to meet his fingers. He tortures me by removing his touch.

"Move and I'll use the wooden spoon on your ass again," he warns.

It takes my sex-addled brain a moment to even compute what he means, but when he leaves the room, I understand. I hold perfectly still as if my compliance with this order will bring me the satisfaction I so desperately need. I listen to his footsteps going swiftly down the stairs then back up.

To keep up the suspense, I don't look when I hear him come back into the room. He pulls my buttcheek open with one hand and drizzles something between them.

Now I look.

It's the olive oil. He brought the spoon, too, which actually would be a real incentive for me to cave. I hope he won't use it on me. At least not too hard.

Dima kneels up behind me, parting my cheeks with the

heels of his hands and lining his cock up. I automatically tense up, my anus fluttering at the contact. Dima makes a disapproving sound in his throat and applies a little pressure. "Now you take my cock, *amerikanka*."

I moan my agreement. It's so wrong but feels so right. Especially because it's Dima. Or maybe only because it's Dima.

For a moment, nothing happens. I'm resisting him, I guess, but I don't realize it until he murmurs, his tone far softer, "Open for me, Natasha."

I don't know what that means, but I imagine opening for him, and my muscles relax. He breaches my back hole. There's a burning sensation, but he goes slowly, feeding his length into me, centimeter by centimeter.

"It's too big," I protest.

Dima uncaps the olive oil and pours a little more between us. "Take me." It's a command, but he delivers it in a soft voice, with a touch of coaxing to it. I knew I was right that he'd never hurt me.

He may play at using sex as punishment, but I'm safe with him. I'm safe, and I can win this battle with my surrender.

I concentrate to relax until he's fully seated, and then he starts moving slowly in and out.

I moan. "It's good," I admit. I tug at my bound wrists because the urge to put my fingers between my legs is overwhelming. My sex feels so empty. So needy. "Dima... please," I start begging.

"Please what?" He lords over me with that authoritative tone now that I'm begging.

"I need... please..."

"Are you going to be a good girl?"

Fuck. No way. I'm not giving in. No chance.

I don't answer at first. He strokes in and out of my ass,

making me frantic with the need for him to either stop or give me more.

"Hmm?"

"No." I sound petulant because I know he's going to deny me what I need.

He thrusts a little harder. "No? I have all night, Natasha. You will definitely do as you're told by the time I'm through with you."

Oh, God. His words turn me on. I don't know why I love it just as much when he's mean to me as I do when he's tender. I guess I know the meanness isn't real. It's a barrier he uses to hold back from loving me.

That's the barrier I'm trying to knock down.

Dima thrusts deeper like it's a punishment for my refusal. It's too much, but it feels so good.

I moan into the bedcovers, keep my ass up, my legs spread. "Please." I beg again without even meaning to.

"*Da,*" he agrees, pounding a little harder.

A little faster.

I'm already lost, spinning into the place of no thought, only lurid sensation.

"Dima," I pant.

He groans, and the sound of his arousal nearly sends me over the edge.

"Please."

"Will you be good?" He drills into me, and I'm incapable of speech. Incapable of anything but simultaneously melting and clenching, ready to come unglued at every seam.

"I need to… I need…"

"You need to come, *amerikanka?*"

"Yes." Relief streaks through me.

"Say the magic words."

"Please?"

His laugh is dark. "Wrong answer. This time's for me, then." His breath sounds ragged as he thrusts into me, and then I understand his meaning. He's going to come.

Without me.

My pussy clenches on air, desperate to come with him, but when he does plow deep and shout, I can't quite muster it.

I dry sob into the bed. "No, no, no, no, no," I complain. When he pulls out, I roll my hips on the bed and squeeze my thighs together, trying to get enough friction on my clit to orgasm.

"You're in trouble now."

I dimly register Dima's threat as he retreats and returns, using a warm washcloth to clean me. He's buttoned his jeans back up, fully dressed while I'm fully naked.

Even though I didn't come, I'm weak with need, limp from being used. I continue to up the bed. Dima takes mercy on me and runs his fingers over my sex until he finds my clit, which he rubs.

I come immediately, the orgasm wrung from me in quick pulses around air.

Dima unties my hands and rolls me to my back. "Like I said, I can keep this up all night," he swears as he pushes my knees wide and lowers his head.

I moan my agreement to that plan when he licks into me. He's masterful, licking and sucking my labia, tracing inside them, sucking my clit. He penetrates me with his fingers and somehow finds my G-spot, bringing out another shocking orgasm.

And that's when things get hairy.

Because he doesn't stop.

Dima throws one of my legs over his shoulder, turning me on my side, and he uses his mouth until I orgasm again.

And then it's too much.

I'm a ragdoll, wrung out from the sex, but he won't stop.

Vaguely, I recall there's a name for this. Is it edging? No, that's when you keep someone on the edge of orgasm but don't let them come.

Forced orgasms. Or is it orgasm torture?

God, I can't even think.

I try to push Dima's head away, which only gets my wrists tied up with my bra again. He slides his fingers inside me, stroking my G-spot until energy returns to my core. My belly shudders in and out.

"Please," I whimper. "It-it's too much." I roll my head back and forth on the bed. "I'm so sensitive. Everywhere." It was true. Every nerve ending was firing. My nipples are hot and tight, my breasts ache. I can't stop the fever that has me delirious.

He keeps stroking but brings his thumb to my clit, applying pressure to my way-too-sensitive little bundle of nerve endings.

"You know how to make it stop." Dima's accent is thick.

"Please," I moan. "Dima, no more."

"*Nyet.* This is your punishment until you obey."

Tears leak from the outer corners of my eyes. Not from pain, just sexual frustration. I'm dying. "Please," I beg again, even though it's just mindless chanting. I don't believe he'll stop.

I'm also not going to give in.

My legs kick out. It feels like lightning striking, sending jolts of energy through me as I orgasm again.

And he still doesn't stop.

"Nooooo," I groan. I'm boneless. Brainless. Completely undone. "No more."

He lowers his head between my legs and swirls his tongue around my clit.

"Stop. I hate you."

Dima goes still, and I swear I can read him perfectly. He's afraid he's gone too far.

I manage to raise my head enough to hold his gaze, and I shake it. Of course, I don't hate him. I'm falling crazily in love with this man.

I watch his shoulders relax. He relents and unties my wrists.

"Is it over?"

"You tell me."

Godpodi. How far will this man go to avoid my question? "Was my condition… so awful?"

I see pain ripple over his expression before he shutters it. "I… can't talk about it with you, Natasha. That wasn't fair."

"Neither is this," I counter.

Dima reaches for my wrists, manacling each one in one of his larger hands and pulling me up to sit on the bed. "Come here."

"Where are we going?" I ask.

"To the shower. I'm going to clean you up and fuck you some more."

I can't decide if I want to laugh or cry.

All I know is Dima has me out of my mind. He may end up winning this battle after all.

*D*IMA

Natasha is incapable of walking, so I scoop her into my arms.

I love the weight of her soft body against mine, the way

she turns her face into me, tucking it against my neck, looping her slender arms around my shoulders. She smells like ginger and peaches with the faint scent of pine and sunshine from her time outside.

I want to lick every inch of her.

And I will.

Because this is the only option available to me as far as I can see. I won't let Ravil or anyone else put pressure on Natasha. And I'm unwilling to use her pressure points. There's no way on Earth I could ever threaten her and still be able to look at myself in the mirror.

Hell, I may not be able to after this, but it won't be because I've hurt or scared her.

It will be because of my trampled vows to Alyona.

And that's why I simply can't open that box up and unpack it with Natasha. I've already done everything else with her. I've held her hand. Kissed those sweet, soft lips. I've fucked her in several positions. I've spanked her, tied her up, had my cock in her mouth and her ass. The only thing I can keep back now is my memories of Alyona. Our bond. Our story. To share it with Natasha seems like the ultimate betrayal, and I can't do that.

I sit her on the bathroom counter while I turn on the water. Natasha's hair is adorably rumpled, her eyes glassy bright. While the water heats, I trace my index finger along the delicate curve of her collarbone to the hollow of her throat. Her nipples stand up in stiff peaks. Since I've neglected them sorely, I lean down to take one into my mouth and swirl my tongue around it before I give a hard pull.

Natasha whimpers, her hands flapping loosely at my arms.

I strip out of my clothes and then stand between her open knees, palming her ass to lift her to straddle my waist.

RENEE ROSE

Once more, she drops her head to my shoulder, as docile as a babydoll. I step into the shower and set her on her feet, keeping a hand at her waist to keep her steady. Her legs don't seem to hold her. She's drunk on orgasms.

She blinks, those sea-green eyes tracking across my chest and down my abdominals to the part of my anatomy that's still thrilled to see her.

I wash, giving her time to gather herself.

"Dima…" she croaks. She drags the backs of her knuckles across my tattooed pect.

Something has shifted between us. I want to bring it back to the dominant sex tease I had going for the last hours, but the way she's looking at me is too real. Too honest. Too raw.

I don't mean to be tender, but I can't help myself. I cover her hand with my own. She touches my fingers, traces Alyona's ring.

I should pull away. I should stop this whole thing. I've already told her we can't do this. But I don't. I'm rendered immobile by her closeness.

"Who did this belong to?" she asks. There's no innocence in the tone. It's not an idle question. I realize, with a jolt, that Natasha knows more than she's let on. Suddenly her demand that I explain why we can't be together feels like a direct attack on my memories of Alyona.

I catch her wrist and step back, under the spray of water. "Don't." I turn her to face away from me—looking at her is too much. We aren't playing games anymore. We're light-years away from what we just did in the bedroom.

"Who was she, Dima?"

"*Don't.*" I raise my voice. My body registers the question as a threat, my heart thudding too fast, the warm shower suddenly too hot.

"I want…" It takes a moment for me to recognize the tears in Natasha's voice. "I want to be her."

"No, you don't," I say harshly, even though she's already breaking. "She's dead."

"At least she had you." Natasha turns back around to face me, and I'm hit by the full force of her pain. Those green eyes overflow with it.

Blyad'. I did this to her. I hurt Natasha.

I lean my shoulder against the tile wall, feeling the weight of three elephants sitting on my chest. All the loss I suffered at Alyona's death seems fresh again, mingled with the guilt and shame over what I've done to Natasha's gentle heart.

And then I just go dead. I can't function. Can't choose. It's all too much.

And my silence, my lack of response seems to send a message to Natasha because she nods and pulls the shower curtain half-open then steps out.

I'm unable to move. To say any words to fix this fuck-up I've created.

"I will call Alex now." There's defeat in her tone. Something I never wanted to hear. Why, in the fuck did I push her to this?

But no, she's not broken because of Alex.

She's broken because of me.

I stand in the shower, numb. I don't feel the water turn cold, or track how long it's been since Natasha walked out of the bathroom.

When she returns, dressed and holding the keys to the Land Rover, my brain can't compute what's happening.

"I'm leaving," she tells me. It's not a dare. There's no anger in her deadened tones. She knows I'm going to let her walk out of here. Her imprisonment is over because she decided it was. "I can't stay with you in this place any longer."

Somehow, I make myself move. I turn off the water and reach for a towel. "I'll drive you."

"No. " She holds up a hand. "I can't be with you. I just… can't. I'll give the keys to Ravil when I get back."

I go dead as she walks out. Turn into an empty shell of nothing.

My brain barely functions, but when it sparks, I try to tell myself this is for the best. I was destroying everything I had with Alyona and breaking Natasha's heart in the process.

Except no part of me feels like this is the right thing.

It must be because I can't think my way out of a paper bag right now that my overwhelming sense is that I've let Alyona down.

I've let Alyona down by letting Natasha go.

But that doesn't make any sense.

17

Natasha

I get behind the wheel of the Land Rover and adjust the seat forward.

Don't cry. *Don't cry.*

I'm not going to cry because I'm so done. Christ, it was like Pamela Harrison all over again. I was sticking around, waiting, hoping to be good enough for Dima, but I was just a fall-back friend.

The kind you play with when you're stuck in a cabin with them, and there's no one else around, but not good enough to be his girlfriend.

Screw him.

Seriously: Fuck. Dima.

I swipe a few bitter tears from my eyes and reach for my phone.

I found it with Dima's keys. They were in a dresser drawer in his and Nikolai's room, along with the pistol. Nikolai had just watched me wordlessly as I pulled them out and shut the drawer. "You leaving?" He obviously wasn't going to try to stop me.

"Yes," I clipped.

I search for Alex's name on my phone, and it doesn't come up. "Right," I mutter, remembering Dima had changed it. "It's under *Douchebag*." I find his new moniker and dial. He doesn't pick up.

"Hey... Alex." I sigh into the phone. I can't make my voice sound bright and sunny to save my life. I'm sure every bit of heaviness I'm feeling comes through in the message, which I think is fine. "I guess I would like to get together and hear your side of things. I'm sort of... confused about everything. Maybe we could grab a cup of coffee tomorrow? Give me a call."

I end the call. Was Dima listening to that? Did he tap my phone? Can you even tap a cell phone? I have no idea how these things work. After seeing how much Dima is capable of, though, I have no doubt he'd have some method of listening in to my calls.

And I'm going to stop thinking of him right now.

I don't care if I ever see the guy again. In fact, that would be my preference.

By the time I park in the underground garage of the Kremlin, I've put up a pretty solid shield of indignation and anger, which I intend to hang onto to keep Dima from ever getting a shot at hurting me again.

I'm done. I'm done. I'm done.

I use my keycard to go all the way up to the penthouse suite without an invitation and knock on the door.

Valentina, an older woman who lives in our building and works as Ravil's housekeeper answers the door. "These are for Ravil," I say, holding out the keys.

Valentina won't take them, though. Instead, she holds up a finger and disappears, presumably to get Ravil.

My gaze goes straight to the place Dima usually is when he's here—sitting at a makeshift work station in the middle of the living room. Of course, it's empty, but the living room is not. Oleg and Story are on the sofa, Story curled onto her huge boyfriend's lap. Sasha's standing near one of the bedroom doors.

"Natasha!" Sasha greets me first. "You guys are back." She tries to peer around me. "Where are Dima and Nikolai?"

I shake my head, trying to fight the blurring of my vision, the choke of emotion.

"She left them there." Maxim appears behind Sasha, exiting the bedroom. "Adrian went to pick them up." He ushers Sasha forward until they both are standing in front of me.

"Wait—did something happen?" Sasha peers at me, touching my arm. "Are you okay?"

"I'm fine," I say firmly, trying to will it into reality.

Of course, Ravil also arrives at that moment, and it's way more human interaction than I can handle at the moment. I hold the keys out to Ravil. "I left a message with Alex asking to have coffee tomorrow. I haven't heard back yet."

He takes the keys, his gaze cool and assessing. "Thank you for arranging it. You will let me know when and where it's scheduled?"

I nod, mutely. It's stupid, but I feel the loss of Dima's protection. Interfacing with Ravil without him feels scary. I see Ravil differently than I did before the night Nikolai got shot. He's no longer our powerful and wealthy landlord benefactor. That night revealed a slice of the criminal underbelly of his organization. They're accustomed to violence. Deadly violence. It obviously wasn't their first time treating a wound at a veterinarian hospital instead of a human one.

Still, he's never been anything but courteous, even that

night when he wasn't sure if I'd screwed them over.

"Thank you," Ravil says and walks away.

Sasha isn't willing to dismiss me so easily, though. "Why did you leave Dima? Did things go south?"

"I'm done with Dima," I say firmly, making my relationship status public. I know Story and Oleg are listening from the couch, and Sasha isn't going to let me leave without something.

It feels good to declare it. Like if I say it with enough conviction, then I won't be stupid enough to want to be friends with him again or to let that stupid flame of hope ever flare back to life.

Sasha winces. "Dang. I thought there was something between you."

"Well, I thought so, too, but it turns out Dima would rather hang onto a ghost than be with the living, breathing woman in front of him, so I'm out."

Sasha's eyes widen, and Story gasps from the couch. "Oh no, was that his hang-up? *Gospodi*, I never knew," Sasha exclaims.

"Damn." Maxim shoves his hands in his pockets. "Me neither. I had no idea that was Dima's problem. I mean, I knew he never dated. We just thought he was sort of anti-social—or introverted. That's why he was more comfortable in front of a computer."

"No." I let bitterness leak into my voice. "He's antisocial to keep himself from living."

"I'm sorry, girlfriend, that sucks." Sasha pulls me into a hug, and when she releases me, Story is there, too. I don't know either of these women that well, but we're friendly.

Maxim drifts away, leaving me with the women.

"You need a girls' night out?" Sasha offers. "We can take you out and buy you enough drinks to forget about men who prefer computers and ghosts to live women."

I let out a watery laugh. "I appreciate the offer, but I just want to be alone right now." Being around anyone from the penthouse would just be another reminder of Dima, whom I do not want to think about.

I make my escape, promising to text them if I want to go out or if I need company, and then I go down to my apartment.

Mr. Whiskers greets me with an angry meow, and I sit down in the middle of my floor, dropping the bag with my clothes and wrapping my arms around my knees.

Mr. Whiskers takes a minute, and then he finally comes over to rub against me.

"There you are. Don't be mad at me." I pick him up and bury my face in his soft fur. "I'm sorry I was gone. I missed you so much."

He meows again and starts purring. My tears dampen his fur as he kneads my thigh with his paws.

"I'm sorry I was gone. I was giving this love thing a chance, but it failed." I sniff. "Don't worry. I won't be trying it again anytime soon."

DIMA

Bozhe moi, this pain in my chest. The moment Natasha drives away, I register it like a goddamn heart attack. She's leaving.

She left.

Even though our end was inevitable, even though I was pushing for it, I'm suddenly blinded by guilt. By sorrow.

I hurt Natasha. That much is unforgivable. I shut myself off from her until she finally gave up on me.

What the fuck is wrong with me?

Didn't I want her to give up? Wasn't that the point of

refusing to tell her about Alyona? About repeatedly telling her I wasn't for her—that I wasn't available?

Why, then, does it feel like I just made the biggest mistake of my life?

I move through the cabin like an apparition, barely aware of my surroundings, or what needs to be done.

Vaguely, I realize I need to arrange a pick-up because Nikolai and I are now stranded out here. I manage to text Ravil the situation then start packing.

"What happened?" Nikolai appears in the doorway of the office. He's lost weight this week, but he showered, shaved, and dressed at some point today, so he looks better than he has.

I can't seem to reply. My brain flips into blank space when I search for the answer to his question.

Like a jackass, he repeats the question, enunciating. "What. Happened. With. Natasha?"

"I…" I stare at him blankly. "I fucked up."

He scoffs. "Obviously." He raises his brows and spreads his hands, waiting for an explanation.

I sink into the desk chair and drop my head in my hands. "Do you think the dead are watching the living?"

"*Bozhe moi*, Dima," Nikolai snaps, like he's pissed at me now, too. "If they are… " He pauses and draws a deep breath. "Do you really think Alyona would want you to spend the rest of your life in fucking misery when you could open your heart to someone else?"

His words fall like a bludgeon on my already battered chest.

I fall back in the chair. "Would she?" I ask. I'm desperate for the answer, even though I won't believe Nikolai. How would he know anything about this? "I promised her there'd never be another."

"You were *seventeen*," Nikolai snarls. "You didn't want your life to go on."

The screech of metal against our car rings in my ears. That night on the bridge when I almost killed my twin.

"You've learned to live since then," Nikolai says. "You can learn to love, too."

My eyes burn. I twist the little ring on my pinkie.

Learn to love.

A fast-forward film of all the moments Natasha and I shared together this week flip through my head. Not just the passionate moments but the tender ones, too. Even the ordinary ones. Natasha making sure I don't burn my eggs while we argue. The way she looked in the moonlight. The care she took with Nikolai. And fuck—the utter desolation I saw on her face when she finally gave up on me.

I have learned to love. Natasha showed me. Even though I fought it at every turn, she kept knocking on the door of my heart.

And I kept denying her entry.

I thought I was staying true to Alyona, but the sense of failure to both of them pervades.

Is it possible that denying my love for Natasha is somehow also denying what I had with Alyona? That makes no sense, and yet it feels true.

I meet Nikolai's exasperated gaze. "I fucked up."

"*Da.*"

I stab my fingers into my hair. "I don't know if it's fixable."

"Get your head out of your ass and figure it out." Nikolai walks away like he's decided his job is done.

"*Yob vas.*" I mutter the curse to his back, but I don't mean it.

He's trying to save me, as only a brother will.

～

DIMA

Adrian shows up later to take us back. He brings his sister, Nadia, to help us clean the place, per Ravil's request. There's no cleaning service out here, and Ravil wouldn't trust anyone but an insider to know where the place is.

Nadia doesn't speak much English yet, and I think Ravil gives her jobs to try to coax her into the world of the living. She barely leaves the apartment, which is understandable. She's suffered a trauma no human should ever have to endure.

At the moment, I find her depressing presence a perfect match for mine. I give her and Adrian quiet instructions about what needs to be done before we leave and work until evening.

When we have everything clean and our things packed, they head out to the car.

"Just… give me a few minutes," I say.

I walk around the outside of the cabin. Every inch of it reminds me of moments with Natasha. The hot tub outside my bedroom. Movies on the couch. Spreading her open on the kitchen counter.

I follow the path from the back door, past the now-dry indentation in the earth where she fell in the mud. Where I kissed her and claimed her in a way that had nothing to do with controlling or punishing her.

I walk past it, along the path we took when we saw the deer. Twilight blots out the last rays of the sunset as I climb the boulder we sat on.

Once there, I sit and stare out at the sky.

I don't know what I'm hoping for—a sign from Alyona? From a God I don't believe in?

Do I want the doe to show back up as a message that I'm forgiven?

Whose forgiveness is it that I want? Alyona's or Natasha's?

Both, the voice in my head insists.

Of course, it's right. I've dishonored both of them. I should've made peace with Alyona's ghost before I ever touched Natasha.

I twist the ring around my finger. I try to call up Alyona's face, but for some reason, I can't quite find the memory. Can't bring it into focus. "Alyona… *mne zhal'.*" I apologize. "I wanted to keep things as they were when you died, but I can't. Too much has happened. I…I fell in love with another woman."

I sit in silence. Obviously I don't expect an answer or a sign, but there is a slight release of the pressure in my throat and chest that makes me feel like I've done the right thing.

I tug the ring off. "You were my first. I will always love you." I throw the ring as far as I can into the rapidly darkening forest.

I don't hear a thing—no thunk or plop when it falls. I don't even know how far it went.

It doesn't matter. It's gone, like her.

It's time for me to move on.

Hopefully, it's not too late.

I glance up in the sky, and when I do, I see a shooting star.

Bozhe moi, I did get a sign. My eyes burn.

I can't believe it.

"*Spasibo*," I murmur to the sky, not sure if I'm thanking Alyona or God. It doesn't really matter, either way. That forgiveness I was seeking suddenly seems to be within reach.

18

Natasha

Anxiety takes hold during the night, and I can barely focus in the morning.

I don't know what it's about—not the meeting with Alex, who texted back and named a nearby cafe for this afternoon.

It's more like a pressure building inside me. The sense of something being very wrong. It's separation anxiety. Like I made the wrong choice leaving Dima, and I need to fix it. Except I have no intention of doing that.

I'm a glutton for abuse, but I've taken enough. I have to muster some sense of pride and not look back.

I can't get any food down for breakfast. I go to the gym to try to work off some of the energy, but it doesn't help.

When I get back, I go through the neat stack of mail on the breakfast bar. Someone has taken good care of things while I was gone. The kitty litter is clean. The trash was emptied. The dishes I'd left in the sink for later were washed and put away. I think it's possible someone even dusted and vacuumed.

Which is good, because my mom is due back tomorrow.

I can't focus on the mail, but I attempt it anyway. I slide my thumb under the flaps of envelopes and pry them open, flattening their contents into a big stack.

Then I see it. *Paid in full*—a release from my student loan. I frown and make myself read the print. The entirety of my student loans—all four of them—has been paid off.

Oh God. What is this crap? Ravil and his microloans. Only this one isn't micro. It's huge. And the last person I want to be in debt to is Ravil. My mother will literally kill me.

Wrapping indignation around me like a cloak, I pick up my phone and dial Ravil's number. I've never called him before, and it seems inappropriate, like calling up the President of the United States or something, but I do it anyway.

"Natasha," he answers in that cool, mild tone of his.

"I didn't ask for a loan," I snap. I'm not usually rude, but I've been pushed too far.

"Pardon me?"

"I never asked you to pay off my student loans. I appreciate the gesture, but I don't want to be in debt to you. I could handle paying those on my own."

"Mm," he says. "You think I paid off your loans? That wasn't me, Natasha."

I open my mouth then close it when I realize what he just said.

"I'm guessing Dima took care of those for you."

"Took care of," I repeat hollowly. Just hearing his name shatters my heart like glass. "Took care of, how?"

"You'll have to ask him that, Natasha. Did you make arrangements with your friend?"

"He's not a friend," I insist. "And yes. We're meeting at the Starbucks on James Street at 3:30 pm."

"Good. We'll prep you before you go."

"Who's we? Not Dima," I tell him. I don't care if I sound like a third-grader. Or a jilted lover. I can't handle seeing Dima right now.

"All right, Natasha," Ravil says in that ever-patient way he speaks.

I end the call and stare at the loan release again. Did Dima hack his way into their system? Or did he actually pay for my loans? Either way, I don't like it.

I hate it.

Because I can't stop the tears streaming down my face.

Dima

I pace back and forth in Ravil's office.

I fucking hate everything about sending Natasha to meet Alex.

"He's an FBI agent," Maxim reminds me. "He's not going to hurt her. The worst he can do is bring her in for questioning, and if he does, Lucy will make such a racket, they'll let her go immediately. Don't forget the video we have of him shooting Nikolai."

"I still don't see why this is necessary. He's not going to tell her anything I haven't already ferreted out. I don't want him near her."

"You can shadow her if you want, just to make sure she's safe," Maxim reminds me.

As if I needed his permission. Of course, I'm going to fucking shadow her.

Ravil remains silent, but I know his mind is already made up.

"I just want to hear what he has to say about what happened, and he offered to give her an explanation. We'd be foolish to turn it down," Maxim reasons.

"So what do we want her to know going in?" Ravil asks. "What questions we want her to ask, what warnings about what she can and can't say?"

I fold my arms across my chest and look to Maxim. He's our Fixer. This is his strategy.

"She can tell him Nikolai pulled through, no thanks to him. Obviously, no information about the cabin or who or how he was treated. She should ask him what he was after and why he fired on Nikolai. Just basics. I just want to hear what he'll say."

"You want her to wear a wire?" I ask. I don't like it.

"No. We're not collecting evidence. Unless you don't trust Natasha to tell us everything he says?" He raises his brows at me.

I trust Natasha. I was foolish to doubt her in the first place. But I can't vouch for how cooperative she'll be. She didn't want to do this in the first place, and we didn't part on good terms.

Since I'm hating this plan anyway, I simply shrug.

"Right. She's pissed at you, no?" Maxim asks. "You want to tell us what happened?"

"No." My arms tighten over my chest.

"You break her heart?"

I stare at Maxim, feeling punched in the gut by the question. Finally I nod, unable to speak.

"You plan on fixing that mess?"

I do plan on fixing things, but I haven't figured out how, yet. I didn't call or text her last night when we got back. It felt too soon. This morning my gut said she still needed time. And I needed to get my shit together first.

"I'm going to try." My voice cracks like I'm a teenager.

Ravil pins me with a sharp look. "She's not broken enough to roll over on us, is she?"

I hesitate but then shake my head. I may have doubted Natasha before, but I was wrong. She wouldn't do that. She's not mean or vindictive, even when angry at me.

He nods at Maxim. "All right. You talk to Natasha— she wants no part of Dima right now."

Even though I knew that, having Ravil say it out loud guts me.

I go to my room, unwilling to hang out in the living room with the living. But once I'm there, I don't know what to do with myself. It feels like so long ago that I was cyberstalking Natasha's on the building security feed.

She was just a fantasy then. An obsession, but nothing I'd ever act on.

Now I know her. I've tasted her. Held her. Kissed her and laughed with her. Now she feels like mine. And yet nothing could be further from the truth.

The place on my finger where I wore Alyona's ring marks the change in me. Everything's different and rearranged inside, but was it too late?

I sure as hell hope not.

Natasha

I order a drink at Starbucks and look around. Alex isn't here yet. He was totally punctual the other times we met up, but I don't read too much into it.

I feel both hollow and heavy at the same time. Sort of like I've been filled with sand. I don't want to be here.

Interacting with any other human would be painful at the moment, but I especially don't want to talk to Alex. He's another one who used me. I wasn't even his fall-back friend. I was just a target he used to get to my friends.

And yes, I do still consider them my friends even if I've had it with all of them. They're still my community. My people.

But maybe he did really care about me. I read all the texts he sent over the last week. The ones Dima intercepted and replied to. He apologized. Said he felt bad for involving me and that he knew I wasn't a part of the bratva. He said he liked me, and he hadn't been faking the good times he had on our dates.

I'll bet that one drove Dima particularly nuts.

I sit down and wait. Time crawls. Five minutes goes by then ten.

Seriously? What. The. Fuck? Alex is standing me up now?

Well, screw this. I did my part. I'm not going to waste any more time here. Not when I just spent the last week as a pseudo-prisoner in the forest for the bratva. I stand and walk out.

"Natasha!"

I turn in the direction of my name to see Alex in his car at the curb. He gives me a wave. "Sorry I'm late."

I walk toward his car.

"You already had coffee?" He glances at the cup in my hand.

"Um, yeah." I turn and look over my shoulder at the Starbucks. I really don't want to go back in. I'd already thought I was off the hook.

"I couldn't find a place to park. Why don't you hop in? I'll drive you back, and we can chat in the car."

The Kremlin is only a few blocks away but whatever. I was supposed to get some answers from this guy.

I pull open the door and climb in. He pulls away from

the curb and maneuvers into traffic. "Did they put you up to this?" he asks casually.

I should have been prepared for the question, but my brain has been too occupied with not thinking about Dima that it makes me choke on air for a moment. "What makes you think that?"

"You said you wanted nothing to do with me but then here you are. What made you change your mind?"

I muster the anger I have for him and wave it like a sword. "I don't know, maybe I wanted to tell you off in person. I didn't appreciate being used, Alex. Do you know how stupid I felt when I found out you'd only asked me out to get to the bratva? And do you have any idea the position you put me in with them? Those are *my friends*, Alex. I live in their building and rely on their good will! I'm incredibly lucky my mom and I didn't get kicked out."

Alex's friendly mask slides away. "You think they're the good guys?" he demands with more anger than I would expect from a federal agent.

That's when I realize he hasn't circled back toward the Kremlin. Which means... I don't have a clue where he's taking me.

"You live with criminals. Murderers. Accepting the goodwill of an organized crime brotherhood is pretty twisted, Natasha."

"Where are we going?" I demand, gripping the door handle. Maybe I can jump out at the next light.

But that's when he jabs a giant needle right into the top of my thigh and depresses the plunger.

I grab his wrist to pull it out, but he's already finished.

"Let me tell you a story about your *friends*. Their *pakhan* is the reason I grew up without a father."

"What?" I rub the place where he injected me. "What did you do to me?"

All friendliness has left his face. Alex looks ten years older than when I saw him last and every bit as deadly as my bratva neighbors. "It's just a muscle relaxant," he says, all business now. "You'll be fine."

"But… what are you doing?" I ask, my head already feeling too heavy for my neck. I let it loll against the backrest.

"I'm using you, Natasha. You seem important to Ravil, so I'm going to see if I can make a trade. Your life for his."

I can't move my legs. Can't make my neck work. As the world spins and swoops around me all I can hear is his voice on repeat: *I'm using you, Natasha.*

Just like everybody else in my life.

DIMA

Fuck, fuck, fuck!

"Right here!" I shout into the phone as I pound the pavement to the corner. I dive into the passenger side of Nikolai's car.

"Where are they?"

"Silver Nissan, turning left," I bark. "You see it? Up there!" I point.

"On it." Nikolai's foot slams down on the accelerator, and he cuts in front of the car beside us to get ahead. "What happened?"

Alarm bells shriek in my head.

"He showed up in his car and said he'd drive her home."

Nikolai says nothing, focused on threading his way through the thick traffic of downtown Chicago.

"You think he's taking her somewhere?"

"*Blyad'*— I don't know! This might be nothing. But it feels all wrong to me."

"He's not headed toward our building."

The brick I swallowed sinks to my belly. Nikolai's right. He's headed in the wrong direction. Everything about this is wrong.

And it is all my fault.

I made her meet with this guy. I put her in this position. I will never, ever forgive myself if she gets hurt.

"What was that?" Nikolai asks when Alex throws something out of his window. The object breaks into pieces on the pavement.

I twist to get a look at it. "Fuck!" I flick my phone up to look for the marker showing Natasha's location. "It was her phone."

"Definitely not taking her home, then," Nikolai says grimly.

"Nope." I text Ravil the update and when I look up, the silver Nissan has disappeared. "*Blyad'!* Where did he go?"

"I've got him," Nikolai says grimly, cutting into a high-rise parking garage.

"Are you sure?" I'm out of my mind right now. "You saw him go in here?"

"I saw him."

"What are you doing?" I shout when Nikolai slows instead of gunning it.

"You want to get made?"

"No." I will my heart rate to slow, take deep breaths through my nose.

When we reach the next parking level, Nikolai flips a bitch and heads back down the ramp.

"What are you doing?" I crane my neck to look over my shoulder in the direction the Nissan disappeared.

"I'm going to park down here by the exit. He won't be able to leave without me seeing him. You go on foot to find the fucker."

Right. Thank God Nikolai is thinking better than I am. "Tell Ravil."

"On it." He already had his phone in his palm, his thumb tracing over the screen.

I palm my Glock and jog for the elevators. I take the floors, one by one, getting off and looking around.

On the top floor, I spot the car, parked right by the edge of the railing.

My heart stops beating for a moment, then reverses direction. What is this guy doing? Is he going to threaten to throw her off?

My phone buzzes in my pocket, and I check the text from Maxim to me and Nikolai.

Alex just called Ravil and told him to come to the top of a parking garage at 7th and Wood, or he'd kill Natasha.

I nearly puke. Alex is off the rails. He may be with the FBI, but this crazy operation of his isn't sanctioned. Just like shooting Nikolai wasn't procedure.

The guy wants Ravil and Ravil alone.

Sounds like… a vendetta.

We're at the garage. I'm going in, I reply.

Wait for backup, Maxim orders.

I ignore it and shove the phone in my pocket. I don't have an action plan, but I can't stand around and do nothing. Not when Natasha is in that car near the edge of a ten-story parking garage with a dangerous and possibly unhinged federal agent.

I skirt around the outer edge of the parking garage, trying to stay behind pillars and in the shadows as I get closer.

When I hear Natasha's voice, a fresh jolt of adrenaline shoots through my veins. I jog around another pillar and—

"Drop your gun, or she's dead."

∽

Natasha

I scream as Alex holds me at the railing, a gun pointed at my head. I can't make my limbs move well enough to fight him. He clamps a hand over my mouth and spins me to face out from the terrifying ledge. My vision swims at the height, and I suck in oxygen through my nose suddenly feeling like I can't breathe.

Even before I spot Dima, I know it will be him. The knowledge comes neither with warmth nor rancor. Just certainty. Dima and I can't help but orbit around each other, even after we've agreed we don't want to.

"Okay, okay." Dima immediately spreads his arms out to the side, his fingers lifted away from the gun as he slowly bends his knees and lowers it to the ground. He keeps his eyes glued to Alex.

"Kick it this way," Alex orders.

I try to jerk my face away from Alex's hand. His palm smells like sweat and metal. My legs barely hold me, so I'm slumped heavily against Alex's body for support. Maybe that's a good thing if it will keep him off-balance. I make myself heavier, tottering against him.

Dima complies with the order, gingerly kicking the gun in our direction. It skids across the asphalt, spinning to a stop halfway between us. "Let her go." He slowly lowers to his knees with his hands behind his head like he's under arrest.

My stomach sinks as I realize he's surrendering to Alex —for me.

"I asked for Ravil," Alex snarls.

"Ravil's on his way," Dima promises. "I followed from Starbucks. Listen to me—you want Ravil, no? Take me instead. Let Natasha go. She's not part of this."

Alex's hold on my jaw tightens, wrenching at my neck. "No, she stays right where she is."

Dima shakes his head. He's twenty-five yards away, but even from here, I see he's pale and sweating—afraid for me. "She is nothing to Ravil. Just girl in building." His accent's thick with fear. "I am bratva brother to him. Take me instead. Just… let her go." He inches forward on his knees.

"Stay where you are!" Alex yells.

Dima freezes. "Let her go. Please—*pozhaluysta.*" He's begging for me now.

Yesterday—a lifetime ago—I would've been moved to see the depth of Dima's fear for me. Right now, though, I register it with only pain. I've shut the door to my feelings for Dima. Nothing will make me open it back up.

Dima shifts on his knees. No, he's creeping forward again.

"You move another fucking inch, and Natasha gets hurt. Understand?"

I note that Alex says *hurt*, not *killed.* Maybe I'm loony, but I don't believe he'd actually shoot me. Of course, I thought he liked me, and I didn't believe he was using me to get to the brava, either.

Dima's lips peel back from his teeth in rage, but I watch as he sucks his fury back down. When he speaks, he makes his voice conciliatory. Pleading, even. "Alex, you don't want to hurt her—I know you don't. You didn't mean to shoot Nikolai, either, did you? Put the safety back on the gun. We don't want another accident."

Something he says must get through to Alex because

he eases the butt of the gun from my head. It's still pointed at me, but the metal isn't pressed to my scalp anymore.

Dima's careful to keep his eyes on Alex, only flicking to me for milliseconds. "What's wrong with her?" he demands now.

"She's all right. I gave her a muscle relaxant."

Yes, and it's made me a confused stew of uselessness. Sluggish heartbeats hit my ribs with sickening thuds of fear.

"Please. I won't move. Let her come to me. Then you can put gun on both of us at the same time." He spares a quick glance at me. "Can you walk, Natasha?"

Alex pulls my body in front of him as a shield. "She's not going anywhere," he snarls. "Where is Ravil?"

The elevator dings and Alex swivels to face it, keeping me in front of him as a human shield. The doors open revealing Ravil with his hands in the air. He's in khakis and a dress shirt, open at the throat. His body language is relaxed, despite the hostage situation playing out in front of him. He steps out and walks toward us, his pace neither slow nor fast, his bearing one of unflappable calm—even ease.

"You're looking for me?" His mild-mannered question seems to irritate Alex, who brings the butt of the gun against my temple again.

I whimper.

Dima inches forward on his knees in the direction of his gun. I catch the movement of shadows emerging from the ramp area. The bratva is here.

Ravil stops, perhaps recognizing that his advance was antagonizing Alex. "This is personal, no? What have I done to invoke your wrath?"

"You killed my father," Alex spits.

Ravil's brows lower. "Oh? It's possible. Who is your father?"

"Sergei Litvin. Do you remember him? Your bratva cell killed him."

"Sergei Litvin?" Ravil scoffs. "Your father is not dead."

Alex splutters, shaking me like I'm the one telling him lies. "He was killed in 1998 in Russia—Moscow."

Ravil walks forward at that same leisurely pace. "Sergei is my bratva brother. He is alive and well in Moscow. Who told you I killed him?"

Alex is breathing hard through his nose, but his hold on me loosens. The gun drifts away from my head.

Dima's crept closer now, and I sense someone behind us, but I don't dare look to tip Alex off.

"My mother. She told me he was killed by the Moscow bratva. The cell you were with before you moved here."

"Ah." Ravil tips his head back in understanding, stopping ten feet away. "Maybe she believes that, but I assure you, your father is alive and well."

Alex shakes his head. "*Nyet.* The bratva killed him, and you were part of it."

"How much have you studied the bratva? Not enough, I fear. You should know when a man joins the brotherhood, he vows to leave all family behind. To the rest of the world, he must be dead."

Alex lets out a ragged exhale.

"I assure you, your father is alive. I will prove it to you. I can call him right now. It is midnight in Moscow, but he will pick up. As I said, we are brothers."

The gun drops to Alex's side, and his grip on me loosens.

"Natasha, come to me." Dima's low urgent tone beckons me. He's on his feet, holding his arms out. I launch myself forward, trying to walk on jelly-like legs, but Alex yanks me back.

"I don't believe you. Prove it, then."

Ravil nods. "I'm reaching for my phone," he says, his hand hovering above his pocket, like he's waiting for permission.

"*Slowly.*" Alex's breath rasps heavily against my ear. The gun trembles. One startled move, and that trigger could go off.

Ravil gingerly pulls his phone out and dials a number on speaker phone.

A man's voice comes on, clogged with sleep. "What the fuck do you want, Ravil? It's the middle of the night here," he demands in Russian.

Ravil keeps his gaze glued to Alex's face as he speaks in Russian. "That woman you were with back in the late 90s, what was her name? Was it Volkov?"

The other man hesitates before he speaks. "Why do you ask?"

"Did you have a son with her?"

"With Yulia Volkov? *Nyet,* why do you ask this?"

"There's a young man here who wants to kill me. He claims to be your son."

After too long of a pause, Sergei says, "Send him away. Yulia and I had no child together. She wanted nothing to do with me or the bratva."

"Liar!" Alex explodes, shoving me aside and lunging for the phone.

Oleg, Adrian, Maykl and Maxim spring from the shadows. Oleg knocks his gun from his hand, and they take him down to the asphalt, while he yells, "give me the phone! Let me talk to that piece of shit!"

Dima lunges to catch me, wrapping me so tight I can hardly breathe.

Ravil ends the call and watches dispassionately as the guys deliver several well-placed punches and kicks, then he intervenes with the mild order, "Don't kill him."

Ravil's phone starts ringing, but he ignores it. Alex pants, staring up through a rapidly swelling eye as the guys check him for additional weapons, removing a knife and a magazine of bullets from his pockets.

Ravil holds Alex's gaze and nods at him. "He was lying," he agrees, like he's soothing a tantruming child. "He forgets I have a son now myself. I'm not going to kill another man's progeny just because families aren't allowed in the bratva."

Dima hasn't released me. He kisses the top of my head, his arms like steel bands around me.

Ravil's phone starts ringing again. He checks it. "It's your father." He holds his phone up in front of his face and answers a video call. "Sergei," he says. "I have your son." Ravil turns the phone around to show Sergei Alex's now-bloodied face.

"Alex," the other man croaks.

Ravil looks at Alex. "You see? He knows you."

"You've made a mess, Sergei. Your son works for the FBI—it's like the Investigative Committee in Russia. He thought the bratva killed you, so he came after me."

"Son..." Sergei croaks in Russian. Ravil turns the phone back around and his tune changes, "Ravil, don't hurt him. Let him go—he doesn't know. His mother told him I was dead. You know the rules."

"I know them," Ravil agrees. "You come here and deal with him, or I will."

"I will come. Chicago, right? I will come at once. Let my son go."

"Call me when you get here." Ravil ends the call without waiting for the other man's response.

He tucks the phone in his pocket and considers Alex. "You see? Your father is my brother. That makes me your uncle, no? We're family now."

Alex leans up on his elbows and spits blood from his mouth. He's subdued, maybe he's sorry, it's hard to tell.

"It's good. I was hoping for a contact within the FBI." He glances at Oleg. "Help him to his car."

Oleg hauls the beaten agent to his feet and deposits him in the driver's seat of his car.

Ravil walks over and stands in the open door. "We'll be in touch, nephew." He smirks when Alex's face morphs to one of utter dismay as he absorbs the fact that his vendetta led him to being in bed with the bratva he so hated.

Ravil shuts the door and taps the top of the car.

"Natasha," Dima croaks, finally loosening his grip on me. "Are you okay? Are you hurt?" With one arm still around my back, he pulls away to examine my face. When he strokes my hair, I jerk back, tears burning my eyes.

"Don't."

"Please, Natasha." Regret washes over Dima's expression. "I'm so sorry—for everything. Can we talk?"

I take a step back, my legs starting to feel more sturdy. "No. I'm done, Dima." I don't feel angry any more. Just so damn tired.

I can't get on the rollercoaster with him again.

Never again.

He blinks, his face pale.

"I'm not going to let myself be used anymore, and I can't be your fall-back friend. Please respect my wishes and leave me alone."

"You're not my fall-back, Natasha. Listen—"

"No," I say firmly, putting my hands on his chest and giving it a shove. "I can't do this." I'm fighting tears, and I really don't want the whole gang seeing me cry over Dima. How pathetic can I get?

"Nikolai will take you home." He touches my elbow then pulls his hand back like he's afraid to touch me.

It feels wrong even though it's what I just asked for.

"Thank you," I whisper. The two words encompass so much—gratitude for what we shared and goodbye.

He shakes his head like he's not accepting it, but Nikolai pulls up the ramp like he knew the plan, and Dima walks to the passenger side and opens the door for me.

I get in without a word.

Leaving the cabin felt like a test, but this time, it's really over.

19

Dima

After lying on my bed staring at the ceiling all night, I stay in my bedroom instead of going to the kitchen in search of breakfast.

I can't be around anyone. I want to throat-punch Ravil and Maxim for coming up with any plan that involved putting Natasha in danger.

Bozhe moi, I will never get the image of that gun at her head out of my brain.

And knowing it was my fault?

Ruins me.

She didn't want to go, and I made her. And look how it turned out.

I sink onto my bed and stare into the darkness.

The worst of it? Natasha thinks I used her. That literally makes me want to shoot my nuts off. She compared me to Pamela Harrison.

Nothing could be farther from the truth.

She was never my fall-back girlfriend. It wasn't a love-the-one-you're-with situation. Not even close. She rocked my world the moment I first met her.

Maybe that's what scared me so badly.

I didn't want her to mean more to me than Alyona had because that, even more than the promise I'd made to her, made me feel unfaithful.

And now I can't even tell Natasha any of those things because she asked me to respect her wishes and stay away.

I couldn't have fucked things up more with her.

The irony isn't lost on me that I wasn't ready to open my heart until the day she closed hers.

I'm not giving up, but I don't have a fucking clue where to start.

I can't hack back into her heart. I can't solve this one behind my computer.

I'm not lame enough to try to text her how I feel. I need to show her somehow. But what would prove I'm not using her? That I've changed and I'm ready to go all in?

I have absolutely no fucking clue.

It's possible I need help. Honestly, I'd rather throw myself down the elevator shaft than go bare my soul to my roommates, but maybe one of the women can tell me what to do.

That's it, I just need someone to tell me what to do.

I head into the main living area of the penthouse, which seems like a foreign place after spending the week with Natasha. It's familiar, but wrong.

All wrong.

"You look like shit," Maxim observes. He and Sasha are in the kitchen in their running clothes with their hands all over each other. "Seriously. You look as bad as Nikolai."

"Thanks." I drift toward the breakfast bar, inviting more abuse.

"So what's the story with Natasha?" Sasha demands.

She's not the type to ever stay out of anyone's business, but for once, I'm almost grateful for the intrusion.

Still, I have no answer. I shrug, weakly.

"She said you preferred a ghost over a living, breathing woman. What gives?"

I shake my head then nod. That assessment kills me, but to Natasha, probably seems accurate. No wonder she feels like the fall-back friend.

"I said goodbye to my ghost," I tell Sasha, my voice cracking. I plunk down on the barstool in front of her. "But I think it was too late. Now she won't talk to me."

Story and Oleg emerge from their bedroom and gather behind me, both of them projecting kindness and sympathy. At the same time, Lucy emerges from Ravil's bedroom in a short robe, baby Benjamin cooing on her hip.

I realize with a pang that nearly takes my breath away, how much I want what Ravil has—the woman he loves and a baby they adore. The whole package. A sweet little nuclear family. Something none of us ever thought we'd have. The women that have come into the lives of my brothers here have brought enough sweetness to counteract some of the stain of the bratva from our souls. I want Natasha's sweetness. I want the whole package with her.

"When Natasha was new to America, she had a neighbor who was only friends with her when they were at home. At school, she was too Russian to associate with."

Sasha pulls a horrified face, always the thespian.

"She compared me to that friend."

Lucy sits the baby on the edge of the breakfast bar, and Sasha instantly reaches for him. "So you need to prove to her that she's not a friend of convenience," she sums up.

I turn to her, grateful for her logic. "Yes. But she won't talk to me."

"So you'll have to show her."

"It should be public," Sasha weighs in. "Something big." Of course, Sasha's flare for the dramatic always comes into play.

But everyone else seems to agree.

"Yes. Public and big," Maxim repeats.

"A billboard," Story suggests.

Oleg signs something, and I watch. It's a little fast for me to pick up. "Something she can see?" I try to interpret.

"Something she can see from her window!" Story fills me in. "Yes! A giant banner hung on the building across the way. How would you go about that?"

I frown. Fuck if I know. If it can't be accessed with technology, I'm at a total loss.

"I can try to find the building owner," Maxim offers.

"What about one of those airplanes that flies with the banner behind it?" Sasha suggests.

"Yes," I agree. It feels right. "All of that." I spread my hands. It's not like me to ask for help. I'm usually the one offering it, but I'm way out of my depth here. "Can you help me?"

"Of course." Lucy smiles. "We can figure this all out."

Natasha

My mother is home, which means I'm in my bedroom pretending to read a book. I just want to be alone while I lick my wounds.

I didn't want to tell her about what happened last week. If I had, she would want to move us out of this building by the end of the day. Me getting mixed up in bratva business is her worst nightmare.

But not telling her makes it impossible to function around her. I'm still grieving. It may have only been a week, but the intensity was unmatched. I fell in love and had my heart broken all at once, and it's not easy to bounce back from that.

An unknown number comes through my phone, and I pick it up. I don't feel like talking to anyone, but it could be a new client.

"This is Natasha."

"Hi Natasha, this is George Engels, head of admissions at the Illinois School for Naturopathy."

I know the school—it was my top pick when I'd been applying last year, but I have no idea why they'd be calling now. "Oh? Um, hi."

"We understand there was some miscommunication with you about your scholarship offer—that it never came through?"

"Scholarship offer?" I echo blankly.

"Sounds like you didn't receive it, which would explain why we haven't received your acceptance yet. Listen, most of that money has already been claimed, but I just had a student back out, and we'd like to give you the chance again, if you're still interested in attending."

"Well, I am interested—um—but I'm confused. You say you sent me a scholarship offer?"

"We're confused too, to be honest. I just got an email from the Dean asking me to look into your case personally, and it looks like someone in our office dropped the ball somewhere. But there is money available, and I'd like to make the offer. Have you already accepted another offer?"

My heart starts pounding. Even though I have a strong suspicion about how this happened, I can't hold back my excitement. "Um, no, I haven't."

"Then we'd like to offer you a full ride. But I'd need to know by the end of the week. I will email you the paperwork right now, so you can look it over."

"Wow. Thank you so much. Really. This is very exciting."

"It is, yes. We were so impressed with your entrance essay. It was really moving."

My entrance essay? *Huh.* Interesting.

"Um, thank you. I look forward to your email."

"Great. I'm sending it now. You have a great day, Natasha."

I end the call and stare at the phone. Then I open my computer, which I haven't done since I got back. My email box is full, and there are messages not just from the Illinois School of Naturopathy, but from seven others, all with similar stories. My application had been misplaced, but there's still a place for me. Some offer money, some don't.

I give a sob of joy. It feels like I just won the lottery. The thing I wanted that I never believed would happen just got handed to me on a platter.

And I know who made this happen.

Part of me wants to reject this gift Dima has given me, but how can I?

This is a dream come true!

I don't know how he did it, but he is truly amazing.

I hold both my hands over my heart, which is contorting inside my chest. Why does knowing Dima cares feel so damn painful? Because I still can't have him?

Yes. Exactly. I don't want to open the door to this pain again.

I know I should go up to the penthouse to thank him personally. But I'm not ready to see him. Not without it tearing my heart out. I still love him too much. So much it burns to be near him. To relive his denial of me.

Of us.

I'll give it some time. Get myself together.

Maybe I'll write an old-fashioned thank you note and mail it to him.

I open the blinds in my bedroom and something different about the view makes me pause.

I gasp. A giant banner is hanging on the building across the way at exactly the same level as my window.

In huge, red capital letters, it reads, *I LOVE YOU, NATASHA.* My stomach surges up to my throat. *What?* Below it, in a script, it says, *You are my everything.*

I cover my mouth with my hand as a flood of emotion threatens to knock me over. Love, grief, laughter, tears—it all rushes out at once.

"Dima!" I gasp.

What is this? Is he saying he *does* want me? A lump grows in my throat.

"Natasha!" my mother calls from the living room.

My tummy flutters. I guess there's no keeping this from her now. I steel myself. But when I come out, she's looking out a different window—one that faces the lake.

"What is it?" I ask.

"What does that sign say?" she demands, pointing.

"What sign?"

"There's a plane with a sign. What does it say?"

I stand beside my tiny but fierce mother. Sure enough, a tiny plane loops around near the shoreline, carrying a banner behind it that reads, *I love you, Natasha.*

"Mama," I murmur, unable to stop the tears.

"Who did this?" My mother turns, looking elated. "Alex?"

"Not Alex. Dima."

"Dima?" Her smile fades. "From upstairs?"

My spine straightens, and I lift my chin. "Yes. He's a good person," I say defensively. "He's fiercely loyal, and he loves deeply. He would do anything for the people he loves."

My mother stares at me, eyes wide. "You're... seeing this man? He is bratva."

"I know." I draw a breath. Until this moment, I was still holding back. Still protecting my heart from getting torn to shreds again. But the act of convincing my mom makes me realize that Dima is worth risking everything for.

Worth trying again.

Without any more explanation, I grab the keycard to get to the penthouse and walk out to the elevator.

As it surges upward, my heart pounds in my temples, my wrists, my throat.

I'm terrified and certain at the same time. I've never wanted anything more, and yet I can't take any more heartache, either.

The elevator stops at the top and the doors slide open.

"Dima."

He's standing there, waiting for me. He knew I was coming. Of course he did—that's his job.

I stumble out of the elevator straight into him. After a split second of surprise, his arms bind around me, and he holds me as tightly as he did at the parking garage.

"Natasha," he murmurs. "Forgive me. I never meant to hurt you, sweetheart. You're all that matters to me. I know it didn't seem that way."

"No," I speak against the soft cotton of his black shirt. "It did. But you also kept pushing me away."

"Never again," he swears "I'm all in with you now, *amerikanka*. If you'll have me."

"Promise?"

"I promise. I'll tell you about Alyona now. But only if you want. Whatever you want." His lips are in my hair, his hands stroking up and down my back. "I'm yours, Natasha. I'm sorry I wasn't ready before, but I am now."

I lift my face from his chest and pull his head down to mine, claiming his mouth.

He lets me kiss him for a moment, then he takes over, grasping the back of my head and angling his face to deepen the kiss. His tongue slips between my lips, dancing with mine. He pulls away and brushes the backs of his fingers across my cheek.

I realize the little ring is gone from his pinkie finger. I pull his fingers away to be sure.

"You took it off."

He nods. "I said goodbye and left it in the woods where we saw the doe."

I kiss his fingers. "I'm sorry for your loss."

He laces his fingers through mine. "It was a long time ago. I just didn't know how to move on until you kneed me in the balls."

"I never did that," I say with a smile.

"No." His eyes are warm as he cradles my face. "You were always kind. I was the asshole. Can I... will you..." He stabs his fingers through his air with a rueful smile. "I don't have a clue how to do this. May I take you on a date?"

I laughed. "A date?"

He winces. "It's backward, isn't it? I've already sucked you dry without giving a thing in return. But...I'd like to remedy that. Can we start over? Go to dinner? Get married? Have little redheaded babies?" He tilts his head to catch my gaze. "Too soon for that?"

Warmth curls everywhere in my body and tiny explosions of joy burst in my chest. He wants me. He's all in. "A little." I bring my hands to his chest, leaning into him. "How did you get me into naturopathy school?"

"A magician never reveals his secrets."

"Fair enough." I smile.

"Are you going to go?"

I catch my breath. Am I? I just found out the guy I'm crazy about wants to be with me. Is it really the right time to move away for four years?

As if he guesses at my hesitation, he covers both my hands. "If you're worried about us, we'd figure it all out— no problem. Of all of Ravil's men, I'm the only one perfectly able to work remotely."

He said *us*. There's an *us*.

I still can't believe it.

"Ever since Ravil broke the bratva code to marry Lucy, all the brotherhood or death rules seem to have gone out the window. He just let Pavel go to be with his girlfriend in L.A.. Maxim has a wife. Oleg's girlfriend lives with us." Dima shrugs. "I don't see why I couldn't move out, too."

I beam at him, wings flapping in my chest. "You'd come with me? Really?"

"Natasha, I'm all in. I want to be with you—any way you'll have me."

I try to imagine what it would be like to have Dima with me at naturopathy school. Coming home to him typing away on his computer in the living room. Watching movies. Cooking together. I couldn't imagine anything better.

"One more question—what happened to my student loans?"

I brace myself, afraid to hear he committed a felony in my name, but he touches my nose and says, "I just paid them off with my savings. I figured you'd want me to go legit with them."

"Wow. Thank you," I breathe. "I hope you don't think you've bought me now." I don't mean it. He had me at *date*.

Paying off my forty thousand dollars worth of student loans will definitely buy me—body and soul.

He cups my nape and massages it. "I plan on working my ass off to prove what you mean to me—any way I can."

My eyelashes get damp. "You already have."

"Come here." Dima scoops me up into his arms and carries me toward his bedroom.

I loop my arms around his neck, laughing. "Where are we going?"

"I need to taste you." His eyes darken.

"I need to taste you back," I murmur as he pushes open the door.

EPILOGUE

Dima

Natasha squeezes my hand as we stand with Nikolai in front of the door to the apartment where we grew up.

I glance at my twin, my stomach a tight drum, guilt and shame crowding me from all directions.

He shrugs. "It will be what it will be."

Right.

He lifts his fist and knocks at the door, then pushes it open without waiting for an answer. "Mama?"

Our mother is sitting on the couch, watching television on the giant flat-screen I arranged for her to win. She looks the same, only so much older. Wrinkles line her face, and her hair is more grey than blonde.

She shrieks, falling backward on the couch as we enter the apartment.

"We're alive, mama. I'm sorry you thought we were dead." I speak in Russian, getting the words out quickly in case she thinks she's hallucinating or that we're ghosts.

Making a soft lowing sound like a wounded animal, she scrambles to her feet, and Nikolai and I rush to help her.

"My boys!" She's weeping already. She hugs us both at the same time. "My boys. How is this possible? What happened? I don't understand."

I can't stop the sob from hurtling up my throat. What we did to our poor mother was unforgivable. How she must've grieved, living all alone all these years.

"I love you, Mama," is all I can choke out.

"We joined the bratva," Nikolai explains. "And they don't allow any family. We had to fake our deaths."

"I lost you, but here you are!"

We hold our mother through her sobs of joy, Nikolai and I shamelessly crying with her.

"Who is this?" she asks, noticing Natasha.

"This is my new girlfriend, Natasha." I hold my hand out to Natasha, and she joins our little circle. "She helped bring me back from the dead." I tuck my beautiful girl against my side and drop a kiss on the top of her head. "Natasha, this is our mother, Maria."

Natasha extends a hand to my mother and tells her it's wonderful to meet her in Russian.

"I'm sorry, Mama. So sorry you suffered."

My mother draws herself up. "I knew you couldn't be dead," she tells us with conviction. "They never found the bodies—*why were there no bodies?* I said. Nobody listened to me, but a mother knows if her sons are dead, and I never believed you were dead."

Natasha gives my mother a secret smile. "You knew," she affirms.

"*Da.* And I always felt like someone was watching out for me. All these prizes I won—that was you, wasn't it?"

I draw my mom in for another hug. "Of course we looked out for you."

"I knew it!" our mother says triumphantly. "So," she spreads her hands. "Where have you been?"

"America," Nikolai tells her. "And we have to go back. But we can move you into our building if you like. Everyone speaks Russian—you would fit in just fine."

I can tell by my mother's face she doesn't love the idea.

"Or you can stay here, and we can call and visit."

She bobs her head, then gives Natasha a smile. "I will come to America for your wedding. Are you going to marry this beautiful girl?"

"Yes," I say immediately, even though I haven't asked her yet.

Natasha tips her face up to mine.

"If she'll have me," I murmur to her.

She accepted the scholarship to the Illinois School of Naturopathy, and Ravil's given me leave to move with her. I found us a nice apartment close to campus, and it's only a three hour drive from Chicago, so I can come back to get my orders from Ravil, and she can visit her mom.

"Tell me that wasn't your proposal," Natasha teases.

"Definitely not. I'm working on something far sweeter." I wink, and she flushes with obvious pleasure. It's so easy to make her happy. Dark chocolate bars and a few orgasms a night seem to keep the smile on her face, but I'm working overtime to keep proving she's not my fallback.

"Are you receptive to such a proposal?" My pulse quickens even though I'm almost certain of her answer.

She gives me one of those adoring looks I don't deserve and nods.

I beam at my mother. "Looks like you'll be coming to visit us soon, then."

My mother throws her arms open and pulls Natasha into a warm embrace. "You've made me so happy. I'm so happy right now." She starts crying her tears of joy again, and this time Natasha joins her.

My mom ushers us into her newly remodeled kitchen

—thanks to another prize I arranged for her to win—and opens a bottle of wine. We catch up with her for an hour and let her feed us. When she brings out another bottle of wine, I fish a bar of chocolate out of my travel bag and place it in the middle of the table in front of Natasha.

She opens it, breaking off a piece, then offering it to my mother.

When my mom breaks off a piece, the ring I had embedded drops to the table.

"What is this?" my mother exclaims.

Natasha gasps. "*Something sweeter!*" She puts it together immediately and reaches for the ring. It's caked with chocolate—maybe not my smartest move—but that doesn't seem to bother her. She puts it in her mouth to lick it clean, then slides the three-diamond band on her finger.

Nikolai nudges the chocolate bar in her direction and she peels back the wrapper to reveal the question I had printed on the inside.

Marry me, Natasha.

She laughs. "Is that a question or an order?"

I pick up her hand. "Please say yes."

"Yes!" she exclaims, eyes watering.

My mother bursts into tears once more, and there's a round of congratulations while I kiss my sweet Natasha.

"I love you," she whispers.

"You're mine," I tell her, planting a soft kiss on her lips. "And I'm yours." I may have held myself back in the beginning, but I will never do it again.

I'm not sure I ever had a purpose in life before, but I have one now—it's making Natasha happy. I almost lost my place in her heart, and I won't make that mistake again.

"To love and to having my sons back," my mom says, raising her glass.

We all repeat the toast and clink glasses, the joy of the moment making up for the years of sorrow, bringing light to our darkness, healing all the places we were broken.

FOR A SPECIAL BONUS EPILOGUE, please join my newsletter and get access to bonus scenes: https://www. subscribepage.com/rrbonus

Thank you for reading The Hacker. If you enjoyed it, please consider leaving a review—they make such a difference for indie authors. Be sure to read Nikolai's story next.

WANT MORE? THE BOOKIE

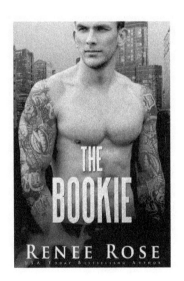

**Her brother owes the bratva money.
I'll take her instead.**

Get The Bookie now

WANT FREE RENEE ROSE BOOKS?

Go to http://subscribepage.com/alphastemp to sign up for Renee Rose's newsletter and receive a free copy of *Alpha's Temptation, Theirs to Protect, Owned by the Marine, Theirs to Punish, The Alpha's Punishment, Disobedience at the*

Dressmaker's and *Her Billionaire Boss*. In addition to the free stories, you will also get special pricing, exclusive previews and news of new releases.

Chicago Bratva

"Prelude" in Black Light: Roulette War

The Director

The Fixer

"Owned" in Black Light: Roulette Rematch

The Enforcer

The Soldier

The Hacker

The Bookie

Vegas Underground Mafia Romance

King of Diamonds

Mafia Daddy

Jack of Spades

Ace of Hearts

Joker's Wild

His Queen of Clubs

Dead Man's Hand

Wild Card

Contemporary
Daddy Rules Series

Fire Daddy

Hollywood Daddy

Stepbrother Daddy

Master Me Series

Her Royal Master

Her Russian Master

Her Marine Master

Yes, Doctor

Double Doms Series

Theirs to Punish

Theirs to Protect

Holiday Feel-Good

Scoring with Santa

Saved

Other Contemporary

Black Light: Valentine Roulette

Black Light: Roulette Redux

Black Light: Celebrity Roulette

Black Light: Roulette War

Black Light: Roulette Rematch

Punishing Portia (written as Darling Adams)

The Professor's Girl

Safe in his Arms

Paranormal

Two Marks Series

Untamed

Tempted

Wolf Ranch Series

Rough

Wild

Feral

Savage

Fierce

Ruthless

Wolf Ridge High Series

Alpha Bully

Alpha Knight

Bad Boy Alphas Series

Alpha's Temptation

Alpha's Danger

Alpha's Prize

Alpha's Challenge

Alpha's Obsession

Alpha's Desire

Alpha's War

Alpha's Mission

Alpha's Bane

Alpha's Secret

Alpha's Prey

Alpha's Sun

Shifter Ops

ABOUT RENEE ROSE

USA TODAY BESTSELLING AUTHOR RENEE ROSE loves a dominant, dirty-talking alpha hero! She's sold over a million copies of steamy romance with varying levels of kink. Her books have been featured in USA Today's *Happily Ever After* and *Popsugar*. Named Eroticon USA's Next Top Erotic Author in 2013, she has also won *Spunky and Sassy's* Favorite Sci-Fi and Anthology author, *The Romance Reviews* Best Historical Romance, and *has* hit the *USA Today* list nine times with her Bad Boy Alpha and Wolf Ranch series, as well as various anthologies.

Please follow her on Tiktok

Renee loves to connect with readers!
www.reneeroseromance.com
reneeroseauthor@gmail.com

Printed in the USA
CPSIA information can be obtained
at www.ICGtesting.com
CBHW021527010324
4848CB00040B/701